Eternity, My Beloved

Eternity, My Beloved

Jean Sulivan

Translated from the French by
Sister Francis Ellen Riordan

River Boat Books **St. Paul, MN 55165**

Eternity, My Beloved was originally published in 1966 by Editions Gallimard, Siège Social 5 Rue Sébastien-Bottin 75328 Paris, France, under the title *Car je t'aime o eternite*. River Boat Books retains the English translation rights. Sister Francis Ellen Riordan provided the translation.

First River Boat Books Edition, December, 1998

River Boat Books
P.O. Box 65314
St. Paul, MN 55165-0314

Library of Congress Catalog Card Number: 98-067820

ISBN: 0-9654756-2-X (Trade paperback)

Printed in the United States of America at McNaughton & Gunn, Inc.

Introduction

In a shrinking world it seems strange that Jean Sulivan should still be largely unknown in North America. The author of some thirty books in France, about half fiction, brought out principally by Gallimard, the distinguished Parisian literary publisher, Sulivan was born in a farming village in Brittany in 1913. His father died in the early fighting of World War I when Sulivan was still an infant. His childhood was lived close to nature and animals, and he was deeply attached to his mother, a peasant woman who knew the Gospel parables by heart. Sulivan entered the minor seminary as a boy — where he immediately became a rebel — and was ordained in Rennes in 1938. He soon became a public figure in that provincial capital as chaplain to university students, as well as director of a monthly paper, a film club, and a lecture center that sponsored such important figures as Mounier, Marcel, and Daniélou.

Although he always wanted to write, he did not bring out his first book until he was 45. Born Joseph Lemarchand, he adopted the name Sulivan from the hero of Preston Sturges's movie comedy, *Sullivan's Travels*. He felt he was beginning a new life, which helps account for the urgency with which he threw himself into his work. "To write," he said, " is to lie a little less." After his third novel, *The Sea Remains* (*Mais il y a la mer*, 1964), scored a critical and popular success, he asked for and secured permission from the cardinal of Rennes to be released from all pastoral duties in order to pursue his vocation as a writer. Although he remained a priest, from then on he lived anonymously in a run-down neighborhood in Paris, producing more than a book a year until he died in 1980 after an automobile accident in the Bois de Boulogne.

As a writer, Sulivan's early ambition was to imitate the classical modern writers of his youth, writers who had been published in *Nouvelle revue francaise*.

The Sea Remains, widely praised for its polished style, reflects this approach. A suggestive study of the awakening consciousness of a retired Spanish cardinal, this book embodies a central theme of Sulivan: the necessity of taking off one's professional mask, of stripping oneself, in order to recover the secret springs of childhood spontaneity and hope. *The Sea Remains* won le Grand Prix Catholique de Littérature, but Sulivan rejected the role of "Catholic writer," disappointing the traditional Catholic public which may have interpreted the novel in more edifying terms than were intended.

A new direction is evident in his next book, *Le plus petit abíme*, which grew out of a trip to India. Recording chance encounters, visits to Hindu temples, past memories, moments of violence, pain, tenderness, Sulivan finds his own voice, more personal and less "literary." The narrator reflects on the meaning of priesthood, and his mystical direction is confirmed by his meeting with Abhishtananda, the Benedictine priest whose French name was Henri Le Saux, and whose ashram drew heavily on the riches of Hindu spirituality.

Sulivan's emphasis on the necessity to interiorize one's faith was further deepened by the death of his mother, the central subject of his autobiographical memoir, *Devance tout adieu* (1966). A remarkable fusion of nostalgia, gentle humor, and lyric tenderness, it ends with his mother's lingering illness in an impersonal modern hospital and her shocking rejection of the "consolations of religion" her priest tries to offer her. Sulivan draws the lesson that one must know how "to surrender an image of God that has become to familiar," and speaks of his mother as having, in her death, given birth to him a second time.

In his later books Sulivan consciously chooses a rougher, more elliptical style in which the lines of division between genres are as fluid as the voice of the narrator. His novels seem increasingly to grow out of a desire to share his own encounters, sufferings, and discoveries. His characters show a greater range: a group of squatters living a communal life in a run-down Paris neighborhood (*Quelque temps de la vie de Jude et Cie*), a journalist who destroys his career and his marriage by protesting against injustice (*Les mots à la gorge*), a man visiting New York to recover from an unhappy love affair (*Joie errante*). There is minimal plot, very little action, and the narrative is sometimes interrupted by ellipses and interior monologues. Potentially powerful scenes are deliberately left undeveloped. Character tableaus are little more than suggestive sketches, with marginal characters taking on almost the same importance as major ones.

Sulivan's instincintive sympathy for marginal characters is especially clear in *Eternity, My Beloved* (*Car je t'aime o éternité*, 1966). The book grew out of his long acquaintance with Auguste Rossi, an older priest who, almost by chance, built up an unofficial "parish" among the prostitutes, thieves, and con men of the notorious Pigalle quarter of Paris. It was this unusual story that Sister Francis Ellen Riordan, who had been teaching French for many years at Marymount College in Kansas, came across one summer when she was in France. She was immediately captivated, and insisted on translating the book although there was no guarantee the book would ever be published. The book avoids the dangers of sentimentality and sensationalism latent in its subject. Instead of an edifying Hollywood treatment of the material, complete with melodramatic twists, its narrative development is refracted by the narrator's meditative tone. Sulivan challenges the reader with hints of an interior plenitude attained by a man who apparently possesses nothing.

The appeal of *Eternity, My Beloved* is certainly not that of a neatly constructed plot leading to an inevitable dramatic climax. Sulivan avoids big scenes, cuts away when pathos looms — "watch out, Sully," the narrator warns — and leaves the reader to flesh out the details of quickly sketched situations. What captured her, Sister Francis Ellen says, was the way in which the drive to express the inexpressible — what she renders as *that* several times in the text — connects with the conviction of men and women in all religious traditions that their desire for the absolute is the royal road to reality.

There is irony in the fact that the narrator of *Eternity, My Beloved* says he originally intended to write a conventional novel about Elizabeth, a former prostitute. It might well have been a success. However, Elizabeth spoke so constantly of Strozzi — based on the real-life Father Rossi — that the narrator complains "Strozzi stole my novel."

After a summary of Strozzi's childhood, the book explains the strange turn of events that landed him in Paris during the German occupation of World War II, where he fell between the cracks of both church and state. The story has an added richness in linking his career with the beginnings of Abbé Godin's work with the Mission de France, which led to the priest-worker movement, and the years when Archbishop Roncalli (later John XXIII) was the papal nuncio in Paris. The central narrative thread, however, connects Strozzi and Elizabeth, before concentrating on the narrator's desperate effort to determine if Elizabeth is a fanatic of if Strozzi's serenity is genuine.

What some might first see as a lack of cohesion is the complex interplay between Strozzi, the narrator, and Sulivan himself. Once the skeptical narrator has sufficiently stalked his prey, *Eternity, My Beloved* explodes into a series of dazzling meditations on love and freedom. Gathering the confidence of Strozzi while following him on his daily round, the narrator finally concludes, "He lives what I only write about."

A consistent enemy of those who would reduce the Gospel to ideology, Sulivan represents those who feel alienated, plagued by doubt but pursued by faith, less interested in the outward forms of religion than in responding to an interior call. In *Morning Light*, the "spiritual journey" that suggests Sulivan's vision, he invites readers to forsake their illusions and become pilgrims on the road to the absolute: "If you're lost in the labyrinth of conflicting truths, overwhelmed by the law, restrained by fear — stop this game, free yourself from faith itself. Live the joyous life of today. Nothing is worse than boredom and sadness. Faith will not abandon you so easily; it's as persistent as crabgrass."

As one French critic commented, Sulivan "did not seek to recruit but to awaken." To an interviewer who asked why *Eternity, My Beloved* and his later novels seemed so disjointed, Sulivan replied that he was reflecting on the brokenness of our world, that it was up to his readers to put the pieces together. "To write," he added, " is to be on the lookout for fissures in this inhuman world, to discover traces, to reveal love where it seems to be absent. God also speaks when He is not present, through lips that happen to be there."

— Joseph Cunneen, September 17, 1998

I have never found the woman by whom I would want to have a child,
except this woman that I love — for I love you, eternity, my beloved.

— Nietzche

Eternity, My Beloved

If I hadn't met Elizabeth near that inlet, among the pine trees along the African ocean, I never would have heard of Jerome Strozzi, never would have met him. He wouldn't have taken over my novel. But Strozzi's name was constantly on Elizabeth's lips. To hear her talk, he was the alpha and the omega, the key and the source. I used to wonder about Elizabeth. Was she a little crazy, someone who had visions?

Strozzi stole my novel from me. To be honest, he's paying me back a hundredfold since he's giving me his very soul. What's good about the soul is that, without splitting it up, you can give it away to a crowd, and still possess it. But Strozzi doesn't like to use the word soul any more.

"It all began like this," he said. I can imagine the whole scene at the exit from the gare Saint-Michel — the clock, Notre Dame, and Strozzi, seen from the back. He has just passed under the clock, he follows along the quay, and disappears into the distance. It's the good season for the booksellers with their open stalls. He hears hurried steps. It was also a time when women wore wooden-soled shoes. He turns his head; his face is caught for a second in the evening sun that is setting the cathedral on fire. And there's the young woman, her eyes bold and timid, swinging her handbag round and round. It all began there.

He corrects himself immediately, goes on: "Without that whole business at Polytechnic, or if there hadn't been that undercover cop who followed my trail, or if I hadn't been stopped at the Swiss frontier, if I hadn't missed the last metro that evening, and if, later, I hadn't been put out on the street, nothing would have happened. You can see," he said, "in the long run, everything is a beginning."

Then he goes back to one of his favorite formulas: "We'll never completely understand our freedom."

I'm glad Jerome Strozzi doesn't like to look back. Urged on only by their desires, so many men are in a hurry to make money, or to get power, and finally, when there is nothing more to conquer, nothing more that they want, they end up glutted, disappointed. Then they invent a kingdom of childhood for themselves so they can be its absolute monarch. It's not a matter of principle for Strozzi; it's a simple lack of interest in the past. I have to drag everything out of him. He's not very good at providing anecdotes. No imagination; he has a scientific approach. So I have to lie in wait, surprise him, reformulate what he has just said. I keep asking him, "Is that what you mean?" It's not at all like psychoanalysis; it's more the Carl Rogers method. But it's not Strozzi who needs to be cured. He's the one who cures.

If all this had taken place generations ago, he'd have been born in a palace in Florence, yes, at the time of Lorenzo de Medici — Palazzo Strozzi, why not? In fact, he was born on Rue Blanche. Until he was eight, nothing much really happened. He lived with his mother. His father, a cotton planter in Egypt, was almost always absent. A great bear of a pal, he'd arrive like a storm, just passing through, his arms filled with gifts. Caillaux and Viviani are among his father's friends; for Jerome Strozzi, they are only words. But the name Dreyfus crackles like a flag, or the sound of bullets. There are inexplicable bursts of anger and unrest, tornadoes that open up deep divisions among the adults. For Jerome, however, all this is taking place outside, far away.

But now his mother's face hovers in the mirror near the door of the vestibule. The glass is foggy. He doesn't have a clear picture of this face; what remains is the sadness, the anguish, perhaps a certain reproach, a look of constraint. The door opens: he sees the sadness in the mirror even before he sees the lines of her face. He freezes. There they are, two feet from one another, but already separated.

It's Holy Thursday. "Go on along to church," she says; "I'll meet you in front of the brasserie, The Paradise." He goes down rue de Clichy. An enormous crowd has gathered. A horse had crashed into the display window of a shop. Four iron-shod hooves in the air, it lies there in the shafts of a cart, with ripped-open pendulum clocks, alarm clocks, and small jewels scattered all around it.

Policemen frisk the onlookers. Then come the firemen, helmets shining. A uniform extends an arm, slowly and solemnly, revolver in hand. The *coup de grace*, and a long shudder goes through the horse. And so the afternoon drifts away. He has forgotten about The Paradise. His mother stands waiting in front of the mirror in the vestibule.

Then one Sunday — the 1900 World's Fair was on. Who would have brought him to the Fair? A footbridge collapsed at the Trocadero; the news was all over Paris. His mother had worried all day. He opens the door. All he remembers is his mother's sadness, that look of constraint.

Was she already ill? Or was it the constant absence of his father? He doesn't know why, but she suddenly raises her voice, a voice that he never heard again: "Jerome, you can go out, but don't go down the dead end street — it's full of chicks." What were chicks? Paper cutouts? Since then, of course, he's seen lots of them. Strozzi will spend half his life with chicks.

That's the year his mother dies, when he's eight years old. No mourning. He refuses to look at her in the casket. Stubbornly. Why? Later, he will almost be glad that she is dead. She would have suffered too much seeing his career interrupted and becoming . . . . And later, if she had known that he was actually involved with these women, living without honor, almost rejected. . . .

How I would like to hold some old faded photos in my hands, to be able to study daguerreotypes, to discover some everyday objects that were part of his childhood. Just by having been part of human life, such things retain the aura of an earlier, shared tenderness. But there are no attics, no photos, no toys, not one memento. Only an old suitcase that Strozzi will drag along all through his life. In my mind's eye he has neither father nor mother. Like Melchizedek, he has no genealogy; deliberately more separated from family ties than a Carthusian monk, without roots, without prejudices. But open to life, and maybe — how do you know? — to some indescribable word that lay deep within him.

Frankly, that's the kind I like. The ones who have no family or folklore. All human hope snatched from them, tossed into the unknown, the solitude grafted into their hearts is so profound that their only escape is flight — or an immense love. They can never be pillars of society — honest, dull, sterile

4

bureaucrats, choked, in spite of their generosity, by the iron collar of prudence. They have such a loneliness in their hearts that they go about like beggars, looking all over the world for father, mother, brothers, sisters. They finally become rebels and, naturally enough, are persecuted.

Why does his father send Jerome off to Geneva, all alone? Some wealthy planters had invited the father to Egypt. He wants to harden his son — that must be the reason. See the world, don't get caught in a rut, become a man. Or did he want his son to become detached from him? Strozzi doesn't remember anything about the trip except that he got off at Chambéry instead of Geneva. A long deserted platform, a giant of a station master bending over him: "This is most unfortunate; a young child. . . ." But the child doesn't feel at all unfortunate; he's enormously interested.

He returns to Paris only to leave again for the Ain, to live with a grandfather who'd been unknown to him before then, and an aunt, since his mother is dead and his father goes on planting cotton, and becomes active in financial circles in Cairo. At least that is how Jerome sees things: a face in a foggy mirror, don't go down the dead end street; and his father a real pal who always arrived unexpectedly and anxious to be off again. Everything narrows down to a look, a silhouette, a word.

And what happens in the Ain? It's a time of innocent knowledge, immediate perception: his friends are the earth — mountains, trees, and animals are familiar presences. Neither happy nor unhappy, simply outside, beyond time. The first innocence. To become a man is to think, to act, to accept separation. It takes a lifetime to find unity again, a second innocence.

When he is twelve, Yvonne initiates him. Yvonne is a little older. It's summer. It happens under the trees. There are looks, touches. Afterwards, they don't see one another any more. Why?

"I wasn't precocious," Strozzi says. "I was in love with the earth, with the river." He was delighted by everything around him. When initiation comes

5

too soon, the poetry of the world disappears. Love becomes specialized, has only one direction. . . . Later, when he was thirty and came back to the village in uniform, his aunt said, a slight reproach in her voice, "Yvonne isn't married, she waited for you. . . ." He no longer knew who Yvonne was.

Then something happened. A breakthrough, maybe the awakening of a sense of being different. Is it the rebel emerging? Jerome Strozzi is expelled from public school.

Class ended at eleven o'clock, but the teacher would keep going until eleven thirty. The pupils got the idea of getting up and leaving at the last stroke of eleven: a sworn agreement. On the last stroke Jerome gets up. No one else budges. He goes to the door. The teacher takes him by the arm and tells him, calmly: "Listen here, Jerome. If you go through that door, you'll never come back." Jerome Strozzi takes his book bag and leaves — it's the end of grade school.

With that kind of attitude, he'd never amount to anything, never become a government official or a bishop, anyone could see that right away. His cousin Florence came back home that same year, no job. She had lived for several years in Russia and was one of the first women to earn her degree in Russian. She was refused a position at the university because she was a woman. Tears on a woman's face are more effective than ideas in getting a young man stirred up against injustice.

So here he is in the Catholic private school at Thonon. Everything is going smoothly. A brilliant student, he excels in math and science, the little that was taught there. As for literature and philosophy, all you had to do was to know what the prof wanted. Organize a few paragraphs, stuff them with this and that from the lectures, refer to the texts, learn how to talk with an enlightened air on a subject you didn't know anything about. In short, to lie; it's a technique anyone can learn. Literature and philosophy will continue to seem pointless to him until the day he discovers that books are born from life, and help people live.

Jerome is highly thought of, the authorities even choose him as prefect. Thursdays and Sundays the students are free to go out, hoping to meet the young girls from Thonon who wear light-colored dresses with flared skirts and hats decorated with flowers. He and his friends name the girls after stars: Venus, Vega . . . . Strozzi sometimes serves as mail carrier for his friends, passing on innocent notes with poems by Musset or Sully Prudhomme.

But there was a traitor. It must have been the boy's real vocation since he later became an intelligence agent. Some years afterwards, thanks to this traitor, Pierre Duflo, Strozzi will be expelled from Switzerland. It was the chance of his life.

Jerome Strozzi is in a room with black walls (why a black room?) face to face with the Superior. The interrogation lasts three hours. "Did he take the hand of . . . ? Did they embrace, did he experience a desire for the act of . . . ?" What do they want him to admit? There's nothing to confess. Just those names of stars. "Does he want to get married?" Of course, later, why not? The Superior doesn't even succeed in giving him ideas. Jerome is sure of only one thing: astonishment. And a distaste for this man who beats around the bush, afraid of words and afraid of life. A curious kind of mentality.

The following year Jerome goes to Lyons to prepare for a certificate in fundamentals of mechanics. Only three candidates — one from Marseilles, one from Paris, and himself in Lyons. At the same time he'll take the entrance exams for Polytechnic. It was during an English course that he developed a taste for research. The teacher had a single passion, astronomy: he was studying Venus. Jerome did his trigonometry problems for him. And it was probably because of Venus that he had given those girls the names of stars.

The same Bordeaux group that used to run Thonon were lecturers at the school. Henry, the academician, was colorless and inanely pious, a man of letters. But Albert, he was really a character. He had wandered around the Transvaal, working as Inspector of Mines; he'd even visited Mexico. When he came back, he was tanned, lyrical, and his eyes blazed. In class he would stride up and down, telling stories of one adventure after another. With a gesture he would tear off his starched shirt and produce a medal. In Mexico, he said, a cable had broken, the mine elevator had collapsed; if Albert was still in one piece, it was because of the medal — a miracle!

It was about this time that catastrophe occurred at Courrières, leaving twelve hundred dead. Jerome had seen the mining villages of the North; the sight of them never left him. It was during this period that people began to talk a lot about the reform ideas of Albert de Mun: "Go to the people!" The idea of living among the miners, as a miner, attracted Jerome. Misery fascinated him, and perhaps also the idea of adventure.

Just as young Strozzi had left grade school, at the end of a year Sergeant Strozzi was escorted out the door at Polytechnic, suitcase in hand. They weren't at all happy, those young sergeants attending Polytechnic. The profs were always away, here and there, in the service of culture, the splendor of France, while earning little supplements to their salary. One of them in particular, instead of preparing his courses, spent his time on his research papers and books, always with an eye to being appointed to the Institute.

One day the students organized a rebellion, put up posters, cut classes. Three students are expelled; Strozzi is one of them. The staging is dramatic and impressive: court-martial and dismissal. Strozzi could scarcely keep from laughing. Nevertheless, he can't help thinking, "A good thing that mother . . . ."

So here he is, suitcase in hand, taken to the gare de l'Est under escort. Destination, Belfort. Finished, any prospect of honors; goodbye uniform, goodbye career.

"What kind of devil is in you, Jerome Strozzi?"

"My devil is many-sided. Anger, perhaps."

As a youngster, he quits school; as a sergeant, he is dismissed and goes away. I try to understand. Does he recognize himself in this child, in this young man? He no longer has any idea of how he felt then. He neither approves nor disapproves. He doesn't judge. I think I can already recognize his lineage; he belongs with all those strong spirits who say NO to oppression. They don't act out of resentment. An insurrection swells up within them, from the depths. Almost in spite of themselves, a revolt against being reduced to a robot, against anything that would entrap or enslave them.

Not for them the cries of anger that are the luxury of the weak who know how to console themselves with bitterness, nor of the eternally dissatisfied, those self-martyrs who, a moment after their outburst, pull themselves together, surrender, kneel down, and make a virtue out of their slavery. Instead, beyond any idea or principle, there is an innate feeling that the person is of primary importance, and that the anger born out of the heart of life is often the only way to break open the path of truth. For what good is it to revel in the truth like a rabbit in a cabbage path? Only the violent bear it away. It seems to me that a person's life is decided very early by a few decisions to say NO.

But it is true that Jerome Strozzi had turned away from a career some time ago. It's impossible to know if he secretly rejoiced in that bit of scandal which actually freed him. A new project begins to take shape at Belfort: he wants to be a priest. He's thinking of joining the Fathers of the Savior. An absurd choice — so many other religious orders would have been better for him. The Saviorites were provincial, rather narrow. But there was a friend, Dupanloup, who had been at Centrale and with whom he had kept up a correspondence. Encounters and friendships will always be more important for Jerome than ideas.

France seemed to be in a period of stagnation. Many believed that there was nothing more to be done except in the colonies. The defeat at Fallière was the subject of café songs. The Saviorites had missions in the South Seas. The missions, the mines in Transvaal, Mexico — all this was turning around in Jerome's head. His cousin talked all the time about Russia, his father about Egypt. A taste for distant places had taken hold of him. A vocation was as simple as that. But what difference does it make? — a vocation is given every morning.

He informed his father, who didn't answer for six months. "You're an adult. Do what you want. Don't disgrace your family. A fine time you've picked to join a religious order. And if you were going to become a priest, at least you might have chosen . . . . If your poor mother . . . ."

10

His father believed there had been a disappointment in love and even had someone make an investigation. He never really accepted the idea of seeing his son wrapped up in a cassock. Later on, he would even miss Jerome's ordination — his ship was delayed. Perhaps it was just an excuse.

Does Jerome remember inner conflicts, debated questions, resistance? No, he has no memory at all of that sort of thing. The novitiate at Fribourg went well. Thirteen months; then the scholasticate, five years. Snug in the midst of émigrés who never stopped denouncing secularism and socialism. I wish I could show him reacting against this victim mentality, against those disciples who were on fire to serve Christ but were even more interested in having their privileges restored. I'd like to show Strozzi protesting against those interminable ceremonies, bombastic prayers, and the thousand out-of-date customs, against a deductive and triumphalist apologetics combined with a mechanistic rational theology. It would have been good to see him catch fire. But no, the time isn't ripe. Intelligence will continue to sleep for a long time.

Meanwhile, his studies fascinate him. Scholastic theology is a prodigious intellectual game, as satisfying as mathematics. Nothing can hold out against it. No way to produce proof that this machine is no longer biting into reality. What satisfaction there is in having such a tidy, exact world, a world without an imperfection, and constructed entirely in one's head!

Nevertheless, when he thinks back on it, Strozzi remembers stumbling over two points: Canon Law and exegesis. Canon law because one day he came upon an article of the Code that stated, "No new customs will be introduced in the church." How can one reconcile that with the fact that Canon Law itself, for the most part, is based almost entirely on custom? And in studying the Bible, the Hebrew language amazed him because of the poverty of its vocabulary. How could he translate it, how could he choose one meaning among so many possibilities? But these weren't burning questions at that time. Strozzi is very comfortable in the rich silence of the cloister, surrounded with respect, perhaps even admiration. He is considered a brilliant candidate; his expulsion from Polytechnic suggested that he might have been a victim of anti-clericalism. Why not? Besides, his mind is on steamships and the South Sea islands; theological debates aren't his concern. Specialists can take care of that. Faith is enough for him.

I kept pestering him with questions about his faith at that time. Yes, he remembers, his eyes light up: he believed in the whole works, serenely untroubled by non-essentials. Examining one's health doesn't necessarily mean a longer life; you are alive — it's as simple as that. The stars and the galaxies follow their courses quite well whether or not we know any astronomy. It's pride, and naivete as well, wanting to summon God to our mental law court. A person believes, not just with ideas but with one's life, actions, the look in one's eyes, the way one loves.

Some time afterwards, however, Jerome Strozzi would question some of his ideas and would hope for the restoration of the critical spirit. For many people, faith has no depth but is only a hodgepodge of truths based on credulity. When it crumbles into dust, it's hardly surprising that many utter a sigh of relief, thinking they've arrived at a new level, found a new value — liberty. "What would change things," Strozzi said, "is to have Christian

12

free-thinkers, believers who don't claim any more than they really believe. Instead of exhorting believers to force themselves into agreement with doctrine, it would be better to encourage them to suspend judgment on a particular point that causes difficulty. That would be more honest and generous. Such a position does not prevent faith from continuing to live, deep in the center of one's being. Life continues. Which is really a miracle."

Amazing —Strozzi, who has ignored books for a long time, here quotes Thomas Aquinas' *Summa*, even giving the reference. "It is a moral fault to believe if reason judges this act to be wrong (I:ii; 19,5). I wouldn't believe if I didn't see that it is necessary to believe."

Completely surprised —that's how Jerome remembers his appointment as head of the theological seminary.

To have dreamed of departures, of South Sea islands . . . . The gift of self is easier if linked to adventure and travel. A young man without any family to make his ordination day a sentimental occasion. During the ceremony, he lies face down on the ground in the white dawn under the wind of the great litanies; then, hands joined, having just received the holy oils, when the priestly "Marseillaise" rings out — "Do you see, my son, your sublime future?" — the lonely young man is deeply moved. Strozzi sees himself already in the prow of a ship, a pioneer of the Gospel, offered in sacrifice — just like in the holy cards.

A few months after ordination, the candidate for martyrdom is teaching at a Catholic high school in Thoissey. Nothing to be done about it: he had taken a vow of obedience. Thoissey is in the south, at the foot of the

Beaujolais country. All the bourgeoisie of the Saone valley used to go to school there, and will continue to do so. To be in charge of the sons of the leading families, and especially of their daughters, is to control the region. That's the kind of thing the Order believed in. So if the school administration needed a math teacher, the Order wasn't about to send Strozzi out to preach to the uncivilized.

"I was a prof there for thirteen years," he says, "alone among all those literary types with their endless chatter." He had to fight to win respect for his discipline and not be taken advantage of. Almost the only one there in favor of precision in thought and expression and against useless words. For him, mathematics represents the most serious kind of communication, the most honest and austere kind of literature, a perfectly constructed language, impeccable.

Picture Strozzi at the blackboard in an elementary math class. The students bring him problems; he writes down the solutions, skipping the intermediate steps. Nearly goes crazy finding the connecting points. His is an intuitive mind, quick to make a synthesis. Like a mystic. Angels watch over him.

He would have liked to take the exam for a teaching certificate for a state school, but the laws forbid it. He likes his work. At the same time he helps out in a parish, establishes a theater, becomes a director. Jacques Copeau happens to be in Thoissey, and gives him advice on his theatrical productions. Jerome works with a co-ed group, and of course there are those who circulate the usual stories. Since he enjoys great authority in the community, he survives. In fact, he is so highly thought of that he becomes the Superior.

Even at that time he had a strong desire for genuine community. Decisions are made in common at faculty meetings — a revolutionary innovation at that time. His doormat is worn out with students coming in and going out.

14

"Treat children as young adults," he said, "and young men as men." All day long, it was his job to console, encourage, or threaten — to find words for every occasion. Later years, he thought, will resolve their problems; what is needed first is a presence, an understanding heart, friendship. Yes, he finds fraternity at that school, all around him, in the harmony they established together. Just as he will find it at Fribourg, where he is named Superior at the Seminary.

I always have a hard time getting him to look back on the past. Strozzi never looks back; that's the previous world. He thinks about all those years as a circle, the future repeating the past, without a break. Yes, he was happy, everything was going well. The fact is, he was living in a shell and didn't know it. Nevertheless, he concedes, there was a certain uneasiness, now that I make him think about it.

He always had trouble with sermons. He gives up Saturday night bridge games in order to prepare them. Strozzi isn't the type that manipulates words. He doesn't know how to lie, and is profoundly aware of the immeasurable distance between what he says and what he lives. He's surprised to hear himself pronouncing words about the love of God, the gift of self . . . . Every morning, when he sees his fellow-priests saying Mass at the side altars around the chapel, as if they were at their separate work-benches, he experiences a certain anguish. It was only a vague uneasiness and he would immediately reproach himself for giving it any importance. Nevertheless, it was then that he decided to refuse any stipend for saying Mass.

His Mass, the liturgy — perhaps he took too much pleasure in it. But at that time he didn't realize the extent to which he was enclosed within himself. He told me that prayer only become natural to him, a true link of friendship, the day he became part of his neighborhood in Paris. It was only then that he gave up his earlier point of view. High Mass, for instance, which

15

had given him so much satisfaction in the old days, when he wanted to polish it like a spectacle, began to be a source of embarrassment for him after he began meeting people living in brutal poverty. With its careful distribution of functions — honors paid to God, to the celebrant, to the assistants according to their rank, to the people — high Mass mirrored a society that was still almost feudal. It thus became a frightening display of the importance of acquired status, the acceptance of artificial divisions, and hence a denial of the reality of Communion —which is an action that says that there are neither rich nor poor, neither lowly nor great, neither masters nor slaves.

Now that I've got him reflecting on that period, he said that he sometimes remembered marvelous friends, young men he had under his direction at Fribourg or at Thoissey. Friends who didn't get too worked up about religion, but whose everyday conversation bore witness to their small truth, along with its gaps and uncertainties, and the mediocrity of their beliefs. Today, though, they act as if they possess the truth, lining up their statements, issuing dogmatic warnings and exhortations. All this in faultless French, perfectly organized and hopelessly bookish. They're completely different men now. But everyone was satisfied. He wasn't going to call them liars. What good would it have done? They were simply victims of their environment, of their education — just as he was.

At that time, however, Strozzi was unaware of any of this. All he felt was astonishment. Anyway, he'd never been one to criticize others — simply wasn't his style. Everything had been taken away from him. He never gave it a second thought. It was unimportant.

What's the point of stopping so long on the classical period of Jerome Strozzi? One phrase is enough to sum it up. His earlier world was made up of the simple to and fro of everyday happiness. He might have ended his life as he had lived it, a workhorse harnessed to the daily round, drowsily nodding in his certitudes, never noticing that the real world had nothing to do with this narrow, familiar fringe that fenced in the world of priests. Once he was retired, they would undoubtedly have kept him on at Fribourg because of his long years of service. He could see himself standing at the right hand of the new Father Superior, helpless in the face of the kindly, almost patronizing attention of the others, which was worse than an insult. "Ah, he's really failing, the poor old guy." Yes, life pushes you on, then rejects you; after all, you must make way for the young. They would have put him with the old priests in the infirmary.

It's funny that they are always left like that, alone with each other. As if they, who bring life, shouldn't be among the living. But no, they are left with the retired, the exhausted, and the dying, since people say that they know the secret of our final voyage.

Jerome Strozzi used to amuse himself in this way, imagining the life he might have had. He was already past fifty. By how much? He doesn't pay much attention to age. He thought of himself as terribly old, washed up, finished. There would be the inevitable honors, a kind of veneration, all the things that make someone look pasty and stiff, and are as destructive as cancer. Celibates living together in a community full of fear. Of cold, heat, and sickness. With no one to hover over them and take pity on them, they pity themselves. Yes, it was all understood, a slow decline into decrepitude. He was thinking too much about death, preparing for the beyond. It is another way of thinking only of oneself.

So he looked for nothing, hoped for nothing. Things happened without him. Besides, Jerome Strozzi tended to mistrust his own insights and initiatives. What happened was that the traitor reappears in his life, the one who, at Thonon, had let the cat out of the bag about those girls with bicycles and the names of stars. Yes, it was Duflo again, who must have kept up with the whereabouts of his former classmates, always on the alert to profit from anything that might come up. He introduces himself as an intelligence officer, says he needs a post office box in Switzerland. History begins to spurt ahead. Strozzi is a little ashamed to be out of danger; there's an element of patriotism behind his decision. That is how Jerome Strozzi comes to receive letters, and send them on without giving the matter any serious thought. There is no danger; religion is a good shield. It was he, therefore, who passed on the plans for defending the Brenner Pass. He should have been decorated. Instead, policemen arrived one morning. Strozzi became persona non grata in Switzerland. Out, Strozzi! Leave your land, your preconceived notions, your friends.

So here he is, thrown out again, on his way to the train station, suitcase in hand. That suitcase, which followed him everywhere, fascinates me. I'd like to look at it for a minute, describe its scratches, the brown spots with white halos on the fawn-colored leather, leather that has become worn out and shiny after passing through so many hands. Oblong, square corners, stiff, a copper-colored metal strap that ran the length of the bag, and in the center, under the handle made of plaited, heavy rope — the original handle had given out long ago — was a slide lock, reinforced at each end by a flat bolt for security. You worked it with a copper ring. A valise that was like one the wealthy used to carry in earlier times. It must have accompanied the cotton planter on his innumerable trips; it was all that remained of an almost elegant existence.

But Strozzi wouldn't like to dally over these trivial details. Two policemen, one on each side, serious as only the Swiss can be, accompany him to the train, offer him cigarettes, turn him over to French customs, and finish with a crisp military salute. I try to understand his feelings, now that he's alone in the compartment of this train which is taking him back to his childhood, Paris, rue Blanche. There are no regrets about giving up a familiar routine, leaving a land of milk and honey, of plenty and peace. He is sick at heart only when he sees Nazi uniforms on the station platforms. But there is an inexplicable joy in facing the unknown, the feeling that something is about to happen.

Naturally, he stayed at the community of Saint-Denis-La-Chapelle, rue des Roses. The Saviorite Fathers run the parish. It is the beginning of the German occupation. Many parishioners have left Paris, along with their bird cages, their silverware, their household gods, their priests. Then, little by little, parishioners and skeptics return: the conduct of the Germans is quite correct — they don't cut off the arms of little children. The priests, too, come back, more than enough to take care of the various parishes. Besides, there no longer seem to be sick people to visit or dead to bury; everyone is too busy watching, listening, calculating, waiting for or worrying about food supplies. So Strozzi walks the streets. The way his arms swing, he seems to float in the air, looking, listening, constantly surprised.

Father Provincial sends him to the unoccupied zone. He can teach mathematics there, or theology, anything. He has to obey. But the German stop him at the demarcation line and give him a lecture: he owes it to his flock not to leave them. Strozzi is careful not to tell the Germans that he doesn't have a flock. Deep down, he is quite satisfied; he has absolutely no desire to cross the border secretly. Besides, no one is urging him to try it.

"Why were you so happy?"

"I knew something was going to happen."

Idleness, boredom — everything begins with that. Girls, as well as boys not old enough to be conscripted on either side, hang out in the streets, in the bars, one place or another. And why are you here all day long, doing nothing? No man has hired us.

Unemployed too, Strozzi roams the streets and mixes in with them. No, he didn't try to organize them. For what? Games? They already have their own. No more youth groups for him. Nevertheless, I'd still like to know what got him to act. "To have something to do, that's all." Maybe an idea occurred to him, more likely an image. "Doing good" wasn't part of his vocabulary. That kind of an approach just sets up barriers. Strozzi isn't one who makes a big deal out of things — they just happen, almost by themselves. He simply passed time with these teenagers, and they laugh good-naturedly at the old fellow, who's fifty maybe, or even older. Through the young people he gets to know the parents, blue collar workers and shopkeepers for the most part, at their wit's end about their children, for whom the war seems only a bit of a vacation. That's how Strozzi gets mixed up with their problems; they tell him about their love lives, their dramas, tragedies, and melodramas: young girls are pregnant and abortionists do their job. In situations like that what is there for the sons of God to say? No more references to dogma and moral theology. Just keep still; that's all you can do. Jerome Strozzi is back at square one, zero. He begins his studies all over again; this time without books — it's a whole different world.

The engineer in him, however, is still alive, the desire to do something constructive, to organize. He's obsessed by an image he carries in his head. Two steps from rue des Roses, on the rue de l'Evangile, is an abandoned factory, right next to rue de la Madone, a real death trap. I'd like to give a picturesque description of the rue des Roses, and play with the significance of the street names — rue de l'Evangile, rue de la Madone — but there's no time for games, and I don't want to distract you. I follow the trail of Jerome Strozzi into these abandoned buildings. The factory went bankrupt at the time of the Stavisky crash. There are thousands of women's shoes still there, but not one pair. The left shoes have disappeared--a simple way to avoid theft. I'm still following Strozzi as he rings the doorbells of the rich. He takes odds and ends, anything he can pick up. Because of the fear of running short, the impulse to hoard was stronger than ever. Strozzi goes from one authority to another to get the necessary permits, they send him away, make him wait; he ends up at the Ministry of Finance, and gets in to see the director of capital funds, a Monsieur Le Mouy, something like that. Let us bow our heads to this scribe, this treasurer, this unfaithful steward — or, probably, to his memory.

"The law makes no provisions for funds of this kind."

"And secret funds? In times like these, what better use can one make of them?"

"Secret funds are also controlled by the law."

"Issue some ruling, it doesn't matter what. It won't be the first time."

"You're asking me to steal, and you're a . . . ."

"Why not?"

Strozzi gets two hundred thousand francs he needs. I accuse him of never having had any respect for money, of always putting people ahead of money. I accuse him of not understanding the value of securities. There is simply no room for Strozzi among us. Not surprising that he turned out the way he did.

Not only can he now set up his workshops for apprentices, but with the remainder of the two hundred thousand he establishes a hairdressing school for the young women. It's ridiculous — Strozzi doesn't have a hair on his head! At the end of a few months everything is going so well that he drops it all, takes his leave. He could have made it his pet project, but he has no desire for power. The factory became a State technical school. By their nature, charitable works are supposed to disappear.

It is seven o'clock in the evening, June 14, 1941, gare Saint-Michel. The group has broken up. Jerome Strozzi decides to walk toward the eighteenth arrondissement, goes along the Seine toward Notre Dame. It's the good season for the book-sellers at their open stalls. He hears hurried footsteps. It's also the time when women were wearing wooden-soled shoes. It's the young woman who was at the picnic in the Chevreuse : her face is pursed like a knot, her eyes hold laughter and a hint of mockery, insolent and timid eyes. She twirls her little handbag in circles.

You only know afterwards that a particular moment in time marks the beginning of something. Lovers ought to keep that moment in their memory like a precious stone which shines for a long time before dying out. A word, a look, a gesture. Places, or a certain quality of light, remain as though engraved in memory, and depending on the mood, the circumstances, the happiness or the pain that followed, you hope either to find these places again or make a long detour around them in order to escape the sharp pangs of remembrance. And when eyes are closed forever, the eyes of those who once dazzled us and magnified everything about them, something unique is lost forever, something that held together streets and faces and gestures.

Who was it, anyway, who had the idea of taking the whole group on a picnic in the valley of the Chevreuse? But what difference does it make? Someone had felt the need to bring the apprentices and their families together. They pooled their ration tickets, the butter from Normandy and Brittany, and had their meal under the trees at Dampierre, a regular feast. Then everyone scattered into the woods.

The young people enjoy being with each other; Strozzi feels left out of it. He goes off by himself to smell the earth, to renew his friendship with the trees; he keeps his breviary in his pocket — he knows the psalms by heart.

The young girl bounds out of a cluster of trees, comes toward him. Where does she come from? How did she get in the group? Who brought her along? Strozzi isn't curious, never asks questions. She says she has made her First Communion — that's what everyone says. What else can you say to a priest? But she understands right away that it's pointless to keep up that line. Even then, First Communions don't interest Strozzi at all; he's approaching the serious time of life. What were they able to talk about? About songs that were the rage then, about new movies. She had seen *Les visiteurs du soir.* "Fantastic, that Jules Berry — you know, the one who plays the devil; did you like him?"

"And Louis Jouvet, in *Drôle de drame,*" she continues. "Oh, excuse me, that movie was probably against religion."

"No," he says, "that's all right."

She doesn't talk about herself or her family.

So now there she is, near this man, some hundred yards from the great clock of the gare Saint-Michel. The evening light, which sets the cathedral ablaze, shines for a moment on them. Her eyes, insolent yet timid, look up at Strozzi. With her left hand she twirls her handbag.

"I think you're nice. May I see you again?"

"Rue des Roses. Come whenever you want to."

Pâquerette turns around, practically gallops toward Saint-Michel. Her wooden-soled shoes go click, clack. Pâquerette — she got her name because she was born at Easter. Strozzi goes on slowly, a little more burdened than before. Her use of the familiar form of "you" was something of a shock. Not that he gave himself any ideas. After all, a poor old fellow, fifty years old, without a hair on his head. Nevertheless, something is happening. Twenty-five years later, he still won't have seen the end of it. It's only afterwards that you know an encounter is beginning.

Pâquerette comes to the rue des Roses, sits in the rectory parlor, on her best behavior. She talks about everything — movies, the Germans (whom she detests), and the women who work for them. Never about herself or her family. If she starts to mention them, she breaks off abruptly: off limits. Strozzi just listens. From time to time they go out together, strolling here and there in Paris. Window shopping. "Never be seen in public with a woman." Had he forgotten those seminary warnings? In fact, he seems oblivious of a good many things. Such forgetfulness will lead him far from the beaten path. One day, on rue Saint-Lazare, Pâquerette stands stock still in front of a hardware store. In the window are these — what do you call them? — these things that are often given to young couples, face to face or head to head, probably Limoges porcelain. I can still hear her laugh, a little too shrill.

"Do you know what they are?"

No, he doesn't. "Tea cups," Strozzi says, the blockhead. That sharp laugh of Pâquerette, I can hear it again; suddenly it breaks off. Doubtless just to break the silence, or perhaps out of a kind of modesty that takes hold when you're about to hear something confidential — you'd like to get away or hold it back, because it can mark a permanent change in both the person who confides the secret and the one who receives it — he adopts a falsely professorial tone: "Do you know why certain cups are white, and others are decorated with painted flowers? I do. The painting hides defects, the flowers cover cracks in the porcelain. In the factories . . . ."

"Dummy."

He will hear this often, said with a sly, knowing air, gently protective. They'll all tell him, "You're dumb, Tonzi."

Then, in one breath, very fast, as if she had learned her lesson by heart: "I'm a streetwalker, boulevard Rochechouart; my sister does the Champs-Elysées, my mother, too. My other sister keeps house and does the cooking."

And the father — what was left for him to do? The father keeps the accounts, he's the administrator.

Strozzi? He doesn't flinch. He asks no questions; nothing seems to move him. Everything is just as before. I follow them into a bar, rue de Rome. Pâquerette pays; he never has any money. I know I shouldn't, but I think of

Samaria, of Jacob's well, and the Son of man who says, "Give me to drink." They're only images, Strozzi's probably already forgotten them; they've become flesh and blood, gesture. But I, I need reference points, connections. I don't know what's going on in someone else's head. Perhaps nothing. I'm on the outside; I can only observe. They go down the street as far as l'Opéra and go into a movie theater. They're showing *Les enfants du paradis*. In the darkness I think I can make out the man's right hand which, just for a second, touches the girl's left shoulder. It's neither possession nor protection, just a rapid gesture, light as a sacrament, while on the screen Baptiste the clown goes through his pantomime at the door of the theater, and Arletty . . . . You have to believe that this hand really did mean something because, years later, Pâquerette would say, "From that moment on I knew that . . . ."

Is Pâquerette beautiful? More a matter of being vivacious. There's something relentless, desperate, in her look. When it's a question of those we love, do we consider the color of their eyes or the other features of their face? No, We simply share their existence. If we stop to examine them, we're already looking at them as objects. To get to know people is, in a sense, to love them less. Sometimes a mother's face can be frightening, suddenly showing signs of age; we are on a bank, saying farewell.

I'd like to know if Strozzi feels hurt when they come to him to talk about a lover, telling him their sweetheart is handsome, ugly, growing old, looking younger; getting thinner, fatter. Perhaps it doesn't matter whether it makes Strozzi happy or sad, but it does seem that they're doing him a kind of injury. There are psychological subtleties involved, perhaps the false delicacy of someone in torture.

I think Strozzi is oblivious to appearances, so I can't count on his help in providing descriptions. Nevertheless, he believes Sabine is more beautiful than Pâquerette, voluptuous, statuesque, but with the cold look of a statue. Sabine was the red of the tricolor. Brigitte, Pâquerette's other sister, was plump; she had the air of a hearty farm woman, and did the cooking. Brigitte was the blue of the flag.

Rue des Roses. The telephone rings. A German voice asks for Strozzi. Then it's Pâquerette on the phone. "I'm in a jam. Can you come to rue Jean-Mermoz, near the Rond-Point?"

Strozzi jumps into a cab. How many calls there have been since that first one!

I can envision the whole scene. Metro George V. Pâquerette, Sabine, Brigitte, three bright spots scattered in the crowd coming out of the subway. They try to rejoin each other, come together, blue, white, and red. Finally here they are, all three, close together, arms linked, going down the Champs-Elysées, keeping step. The crowd parts in front of them, arms stretch out, a procession forms. They go past the bar du Colisée, and everything gets worse. The customers stand and applaud. People start to sing "La Marseillaise" — "Allons enfants de la patrie . . . ." There are shrill whistles. Two policemen of the Wehrmacht appear, enormous medals on their chest, prize-winning bulls. The tricolor is broken up by the green-gray. The girls are taken to the police station. Everything becomes silent; the side streets are suddenly deserted.

When Strozzi arrives at rue Mermoz, the three are huddled in a corner, as shy as high school girls, terrified. They have a good sense of theater. The officer is very correct, gives Strozzi a military salute. After all, he is for religion . . . .

"Monsieur le Curé knows these young women?"

"Of course, they're parishioners, good parishioners. A little young, perhaps, a little mischievous."

"Ja, ja." Just as he had thought, the German says, adolescent pranks. He just wanted to be confirmed in his own impressions. "Ach, die pariser Madchen! Ah, these Parisian girls, these Parisian girls!" It was a full absolution.

Strange sort of parishioners, who live in Vanves beyond the market. Anyway, that's how Strozzi met the other children in the family.

In Vanves the family lives in a tidy one-story house. No one could have any suspicion. No man ever crosses their door. Champs-Elysées, Clichy, that's one world; Vanves is another. Here everything is the soul of respectability. A statue of Our Lady of Lourdes on the mantle, flowers on the table. They listen to Radio-London. For two years Strozzi is a frequent visitor at Vanves.

The first time it was by surprise. It seems that what he does best is always in spite of himself. When he knocked, everyone was around the set listening

28

to the radio. He could have sworn it was the BBC. There were sounds of hurried footsteps, a jamming of the broadcast, then the sound of Edith Piaf:

Le ciel est bleu
La mer est verte
Laisse un peu
La fenêtre ouverte . . . .

"Don't be afraid," Strozzi said, his back against the night. Strozzi was exhausted that evening. What was he doing? Still busy with his workshops on rue de l'Evangile? In any case, he had to do more canvassing. Besides, he had been assigned a worker's job. Official work. His friend Abbé Godin was preparing a report that would cause quite a stir. That evening, at the end of a long day, Strozzi had had a long talk with Godin. They could hardly admit, maybe, that their work was weighing on them. But there was something in the air; you could sense it everywhere, an enthusiasm. Something was going to happen for these men, who were tired of being considered civic leaders and were fed up with pious phrases. They'd had enough of providing moral comfort; they were on fire to leave the institutional fortress and go out unarmed.

Strozzi, reeling from fatigue, dizzy with hope, collapses into the last metro train of the night. When he wakes up, he thinks he's at La Chapelle, but the station is Porte de Versailles. It's midnight, there are no more trains, curfew. As usual, he doesn't have any money. Besides, it would be impossible to find a cab. Of course, he could go to the nearest police station and ask for a pass, but the idea is repugnant to him. So he goes to Vanves, knocks on the door.

They make a celebration out of it; he had saved the girls from the Gestapo. The story had already taken on heroic proportions. So the family gathers around the table. Flowers, Our Lady of Lourdes on the mantel. Everyone seems to be lovingly affectionate. Is something going on in Strozzi's head? But he doesn't spend his time thinking. He never explains himself. What

29

did they all talk about until morning? About Radio-London, rationing, the Nazis. The father tells stories about the war. No mention of the kind of work they do. But then, the rich don't speak very much about their deals, either. Brigitte comes in from the kitchen.

"Go get a chair, Pâquerette," the mother says.

Please note, now, two years have gone by in a flash. All this time Jerome Strozzi has been seeing the family once or twice a month. Radio-London, DeGaulle, Marshal Petain — they talked about everything. Except the profession . . . . Pâquerette was married just this morning in church. Married a foreman at Panhard's. Sabine had gotten married three months earlier. She now lives in sunny Perpignan, and is quite happy. It's almost a year since Pâquerette and her mother quit their profession. The father has taken up his former trade again — he's a cobbler. Brigitte still does the cooking. Pâquerette's husband, whose name is Adrian, doesn't have any family. Which is convenient.

Here they are at the wedding table, Adrian and the whole family, minus Sabine in Perpignan, plus Strozzi. Pâquerette is in high spirits, as usual a bit shrill, with a few bursts of nostalgia. She recalls the past — that is, the past she can talk about: the pub at Dampierre, the *Marseillaise*, the Champs-Elysées — "Remember, Strozzi? Remember the first night we spent together?"

A terrible silence falls on the group, just as it would in any respectable family. Pâquerette just wanted to talk about that first evening when he had made a mistake about the Metro stop and had come to their home.

"Pâquerette, go get a chair," her mother had said.

"Think of it," Pâquerette says to Strozzi, "there you were, sitting on my chair, me on your lap. Everyone thought it was only natural. We talked until it was time for the first Metro."

I'm trying to understand the confidence born in Pâquerette, which grows, becomes contagious. The first man with whom she had ever walked and talked who did not brush against her and touch her, did not try to deceive her, and did not lecture her — which is really just another way to touch and deceive you, and treat you like an object. The first man who had ever looked at her as a human being. She doesn't say all these fine words to herself, everything develops in obscurity, doubtless mixed up with quite ordinary feelings: possibly she's thinking of a calendar painting of a newly married bride and a house, and at the same time of Strozzi's friendship and God's love — why not? And if she sat on Strozzi's lap that night, it must have been entirely innocent. Or is she, without knowing it, looking for a proof, is she tempting the devil? Everything probably starts from this point: self-respect becomes possible again.

The regeneration of the whole family — it's a little too much, a story-book ending. In any case, Strozzi comes to Vanves for two years on monthly or bimonthly visits. What can it all amount to? Ultimately, there is only one meeting. I myself for fifteen years went to see my mother every Sunday, and in my memory now I saw her only once. Only that one farewell.

Just as I used to kiss my mother, he kisses them on their forehead: Pâquerette, Sabine, who has to lean down a little when she's wearing high heels, their mother — and, why not? Brigitte, the cook.

"What did you talk about, Strozzi? What did you talk about?"

"Nothing, I told you, nothing. The radio, the Occupation, finding enough food."

Never a word about the profession. Does Strozzi have anything to do with what took place? Well, yes. He helped Adrian and Pâquerette find an apartment at Montreuil. The landlady wanted someone to co-sign the lease immediately; can't miss a day's rent. "I'm their uncle," Strozzi says, "I'll sign." Tonton Strozzi — too hard to pronounce. It became Tonzi. The name stuck.

Wisdom, common sense, find it hard to accept all this. I'm determined not to be taken in so easily. I believe in the mechanisms of desire, which operate within us without our knowing it, and set the whole machine in motion. I'm vulnerable, modern. In spite of myself I have the idea that everything is explained by our lower nature. I examine things closely, I always stay on the look-out; I like to see the lie flushed out of its hiding place. That's when I experience real satisfaction, immediately clouded over by a certain sadness; at the same time I'm seized by the crazy hope of stumbling upon the inexplicable. Inquisitor that I am, maybe I'm praying for the impossible to be true.

Tonzi, the girl on his lap, the pious family — the picture irritates me; I can imagine the snickers if they tried to put the scene in a movie. As if that were the criterion! But in the end Tonzi gets on my nerves with that serenity of his.

"Tonzi, are you a man? What about 'the near occasions of sin'? How do you account for your virtue?"

"I see that you still remember the old vocabulary," Strozzi says. "I don't know; I can't explain it. If you want, it's just a question of a little girl on her grandfather's lap. Or maybe you're obsessed with sex, too, like our celebrated Catholic writer . . . . Or maybe it's just my nature."

Je suis ce que je suis.

Est-ce ma faute à moi?

"I am what I am, is that my fault?" He's parodying Edith Piaf. He laughs. Not the kind of laugh people use when they're trying to escape, a way of covering their tracks, but the hearty laugh of a completely free man. He looks at me as if from another shore. So I have to work out an interpretation all by myself. Thirty years of fidelity, inner discipline, prayer--perhaps that's enough to explain it all. Let's see now: he was a little more than fifty when he met Pâquerette and her sisters, and through them, any number of women. At fifty are the passions . . . ? But what about the noonday devil? The fears that come when life speeds up and begins to sputter like a fuse on the point of going out. The sudden panic.

"Perhaps I do need women. I think that a man, in order to be a man, has to meet a woman who will bind him to the world . . . ."

Ah, he's going to confess, I'm familiar with this kind of silence, which becomes even deeper when truth is about to break out and light up everything. I swallow hard. But no, it's not what I expected.

"Why does it necessarily have to be knowing in the flesh? You'd like it if I'd say . . . Well yes, I have felt some — what do you call them, desires, impulses? — like everyone else. Only, there has always been something stronger than desire, a question: how could I, Strozzi, be of service to all the others? Don't laugh. One woman isn't enough for me. That's it — I want to be available, free. For me, you see, the sexual relationship has a metaphysical value. It's a pledge, a commitment. I feel it in my flesh. It's not a moral idea, not a law, but a basic fact."

Tonzi is suffering. I can see it. Words can't express the most finely-tuned, delicate aspects of existence. He remembers one time when one of the women, just in fun, had kissed him on the mouth.

"Do you know what that means?" she had said.

"Yes," he had answered, "a kiss wants to capture the thoughts of the one who is embraced, since all thoughts pass through the mouth." He was quoting St. Francis de Sales' Treatise on the Love of God.

She had laughed and said, "You're so dumb. It means that you want . . . ."

"That's what you think," Strozzi had said, "but not me."

I'd like to ask him about Gisèle. I hesitate, held back by a sense of propriety. A doctor had told me the story.

Gisèle was in the hospital at Belhomme. Every time a doctor, a priest, or no matter who, would come into her room, she would begin to take off her clothes and say, "Would you like to sleep with me?" Then she would become delirious; treatment seemed impossible. Chaplains attributed her problem to the presence of the devil and refused to enter the room. So the director of Belhomme telephones Strozzi:

"Are you afraid of seeing a naked woman?"

"No."

Tonzi goes to see her. Gisèle orders tea. The nurse brings the tea set, and goes out. Gisèle gets up and begins to undress.

"Do you want to sleep with me?"

"Yes."

She trembles all over; then her face lights up. She sits down, serves tea. She has forgotten everything. The Director and the nurses are listening at the door; nothing but calm conversation. Suddenly the tears come: Gisèle talks and talks. Strozzi doesn't say a word. Gisèle's treatment can begin. The crises of delirium have disappeared.

"But what would you have done if she had actually wanted to go to bed with you?", the Director asked.

"I don't know. Why ask pointless questions?"

Tonzi affirms the person — that's about as close as you can get to it. Anyone, he says, could have done as much.

Whatever became of Sabine and Pâquerette? I was eager to find out. It turned out as bad as it could be. They've forgotten everything. They've become conformists, rigid moralists. Incredibly demanding with their children, finicky about where they go, the company they keep. They don't realize it, but they're turning the kids into little rebels. As for Tonzi, they no longer understand him. How could he go on living among all those . . . ? Sabine had even become a lay catechist in her parish. They would have been so pleased if Strozzi had settled down and become a good priest. But Strozzi bolted.

I wanted to hear him say that it would have been better to have left them in their original situation. Impossible; he only says what he means. Tonzi doesn't judge. "There are so many paths through life," he reminds me. "To the person you pulled out of a bad situation, you'll always be associated with that rotten period, so he may no longer want to see you."

Strozzi was someone from their past, and they rejected him along with that past. Very well. Many people need conventions in order to protect themselves. Jerome says he hadn't understood anything about the bourgeoisie, about their fears and prejudices, until he saw what the best of these young women became. It's an idea to which he will often return.

"The prodigal son, the fatted calf, the music — that's all fine. But what becomes of the prodigal son afterwards?"

"Still, there's Elizabeth. Without her, Tonzi, I'd never have met you."

"Oh yes, Elizabeth. Well, you know better than I what she became."

Now I'm going to tell Elizabeth's story. I'm not really abandoning Strozzi. Elizabeth was supposed to be the main character of my novel. I would have liked a neat plot line, a tight, effective trap, above all, invisible. That's what people really like — to be taken in. I had the whole story in my head: the important thing was to make it logical, true to life. As if life were logical! As if to write doesn't mean living more intensely, all the while grasping that special quality which has been born from life, which has been nourished and transformed in the crucible of the soul and escapes in an irretrievable moment.

Life crossed me up, because I met Elizabeth this spring at Taussat. She had quit the profession, and was living in a bungalow, 1925-style, called La Cagouille. Her father, who was as interested in words as he was in pendulum clocks and alarm clocks, had given it that name. It was just a bungalow with a doll's house verandah, a simple overhanging roof with festoons that made a circumflex accent above the door. Could she ever have dreamed that she would come here to live out her life? She never believed she'd leave those barren Paris streets, and what people usually call the "hot" quarter. And now every morning when she pushed open the shutters, she was opening a door quivering with dawn, unfolding the blue of the sky. The trees encircled her with their arms like a protective power that arose from the very depths of her being.

Taussat: at different times of the day every house has the sea in its garden, with boats waiting at the shore. You wake up at night and it's high tide: you hear the suction of the tide on the flatboat and say to yourself, "There it is." You go outside in your pajamas to look at the sea in your garden, to hear the swish-swash. That does it: into the boat, take the oars, go for a ride under the stars. Taussat: on one side, there's the inlet, with its powerful smell of seaweed and decay as the tide goes out, and comes in again. The inlet has a secret sadness; its tasteless villas all look alike, giving the impression that they gave birth to a matching series — My Dream, Not Enough, We Two. On the other side, pine trees as far as the eye can see, crippled from being bled white, and paths with miles of solitude. Here and there one spies, perched in the fork of a tree, tiny shelters that are used by hunters of wild ducks and pigeons.

Only the sound of airplanes breaks the silence, wounding everything that lives, a warning that evil is never idle. Only ten minutes away by car. Here are the warriors of the outpost, trees on the edge of wooded dunes, sacrificed to hold the conquered land, tortured by an all-powerful wind: a wind that skims the ground, lashes out, curves around, and makes the grass stand straight up. Suddenly, before you've even reached the top of the last little hill, before you've even seen anything, you hear the drums of the sea that set your blood coursing to their beat, a great triumphal roar; then you pass the last headlong steps and there you are, standing all alone, rooted in the wind at the edge of eternity.

There is the ocean, purifying, keeping intact ten, twenty, thirty kilometers of sand, stretching out to the infinite, to the shores of Africa. You walk along the sea, opalescent, foaming, roaring, whipped by a force not within but beyond it, that swells, bends, scatters, hurls its spray and bits of foam, rises once more, collapses, and then comes together again, like thoughts that are composed and then dissolve in one's head, rush out of control in a sudden rush of panic, but begin to grow calm as every so often the sun traces a golden path dancing toward the open sea.

Dazzled by it all, Elizabeth walked near the inlet, among the pines, or along the ocean. And while she was telling her incredible story, after long silences as we walked close to the booming rush of the waves that render all words ridiculous, I tried to discover a rhythm, an inner breathing, a heartbeat. Only by getting her story down in writing would I find out if the impossible were true, if Elizabeth really had existed.

But Strozzi would always come back into it. To hear Elizabeth tell it, he was the beginning of it all, the reason and the key, the alpha and the omega.

If I close my eyes, the first thing I hear is the creaking of a stairway under a man's heavy footsteps. Everything starts with that. The paint on the walls is flaking; you can hardly make them out in the half-light. Two thirty-watt bulbs throw off a halo of dirty yellow light, like those in books that describe rooms dedicated to cheap vice. Pigalle is all around: its rhythm, the murmur of its traffic persist in the man's head. Then the bedroom — which you can make out more clearly — it's almost ascetic. The floor must have been bleached, scoured almost white, scraped until long splinters appeared. A large black metal bed. Possibly a cotton bedspread with faded flowers, pink or blue, or maybe they don't bother about bedspreads in these rooms that are rented for an hour or less. Functional.

Images flicker over the man's distraught face and no longer reach his heart. The woman is almost undressed already. Does he even see her? He has sat down. Short-legged, long-waisted, his right hand on his umbrella, the other holding his gloves placed on his left leg. Broad back, long face, egg-shaped head, sparse black hair slicked down with a wide part. In short, a carefully groomed, even a meticulous gentleman. Life can be very upsetting but we go on repeating long-established routines: straighten the bow tie; one doesn't go out without gloves and an umbrella.

In the meantime she's repeating her lesson: because for a long time now, there has been only one man, attached to no particular face:

"Well, are you going to undress or not? Hurry up. It's for a half hour; if more, the price doubles. You have to pay in advance."

What can she offer this man who is so tidy? A worn out towel, some soap? The man hangs his umbrella on the bedstead, keeps his gloves in his left hand, and with the right takes out a billfold bulging with crisp new hundred franc bills. He looks as if he's going to hand over the whole bundle.

"What do you want from me for that much money? Easy to see you don't know much about this business. Here, two hundred francs is enough."

"I'm not interested in . . . . It isn't that you — on the contrary, but . . . ."

"What, are you one of those kinky types? What will people like you think of next?"

"One time" — but now she's no longer talking to the client; it's later at Taussat that she will tell this story — "one time I went up to the room with a young fellow who had a beard, a Jesus-type, his eyes blazing. He had me stretch out on the bed and he just stayed there looking out the window. . . . Well, he'd paid his money, so . . . . He would close one eye, then the other; he curved his hand into the form of a spyglass, like painters do — you know, I've posed as a model at La Grande Chaumière. He looked harmless enough, and I fell asleep, would you believe it? I had a nightmare; I was dreaming that a man was strangling me. I woke up and he had covered me with a sheet like in a mortuary. He was holding my hand, and looking at me with a terrible pity. He was crying, the fool, and I began to scream. Now I know why: it was because of Alexander; he had the same gentleness in his eyes.

"'Get out of here,' I yelled. 'I hate pity; I prefer being hit.'"

"'I was afraid you'd catch cold,' he stammered."

"I don't know why I'm telling you all this."

"You're going to catch cold, Madame," the man said. "I only wanted to try to understand . . . ."

"You are a . . . what are you, really?"

It was then that she saw the tears rolling noiselessly down his cheeks. There he was, clumsily holding out the soap and towel. She knelt down, took the towel, and wiped his face.

"What's the matter, mon petit père?"

That's the way my novel went.

Then she would leave the profession, she would have a complete change of heart. Time would flow backwards. What I want to know is: what happens in that instant when everything falls apart, when there's a crack in eternity? Her father had died, like millions of others, in a camp in Germany, the same year her daughter was born, the child of the Saint-Cyr second lieutenant. Alexander had tried to get to England, but failed. Rumor had it that he had turned against the Resistance. He had met up with a colonel recruiting for the Germans and had enlisted for the Eastern front. She thought he was in London; he was actually in Berlin. Ready to fight any place, it didn't matter, as long as history doesn't pass him by. His head had been filled with pictures of battles and heroism. Or maybe he had a passion for death . . . .

No, reality was less beautiful. Alexander was able to stay with her for hours, just holding her hand; she read adoration on his face. How could she have known that desire takes all forms, even that of renunciation and infinite patience? Elizabeth had found love, that "dark and tender love" — yes, she'd read the poets . . . . Flesh doesn't have all that much importance, he used to say; it should never be allowed to dominate our lives. That was his only moral law, he said, real morality; the rest was simply a matter of social convention, formalities. The union of two bodies comes only as a surprise; impossible to prevent, it was a prize carried off because of the ecstasy of two souls. They must on no account allow the flesh to become too important.

Elizabeth didn't hear his words, she was listening to the sound of a voice. A mystic, a kind of saint, that's what Alexander was in her eyes. Undoubtedly, he was only keeping his distance, preparing his withdrawal, turning circumstances to account; clever at lying sincerely, he made use of lofty sentiments.

He had gone home to spend a few months with his family. She realized she was pregnant, was almost happy about it, and had written him. He had answered that it would, of course, be a great happiness, but after all, there was a war going on. Of course, it would be wrong for him, a Catholic, to advise her to . . . . He would come to Paris. After that he delayed, then promised to come but never arrived. She took the train for Laval. I can see her in this train crowded with heroes who were going to the country in search of good butter and fat chickens; and I can imagine the return trip, sitting next to the fowl, with the train stopping for hours in open country.

The house, whose owners were obviously well off, was deserted; they had left the lovers alone. It is in this bourgeois salon, whose shutters were closed and in which the chandeliers were lighted even though it was noon, that Elizabeth experienced real horror. She was overwhelmed by armchairs, doilies, bride's bouquets under glass, knick-knacks, and an ivory Christ on an ebony cross above the fireplace.

Alexander was striding up and down the great rococo salon, smoking one cigarette after another. This was not the man she had known, but someone who was nervous, impatient, hard. She had noticed the way he looked at her, and it destroyed her. A child? Absolutely not. He wanted no trace left behind. Besides, how could he be certain that . . . ? Well, what proof did he really have that it was his? He could give her the address of a doctor in Paris. Things like this were done every day; he had read the statistics. With a war going on, people wouldn't pay very close attention to one death more or less.

Arguments had been followed by anger. When she timidly tried to speak the language of love, he screamed, "No high-flown sentiments, please!" She could take the next train. Musn't miss it; his parents would be coming back any minute. She suspected they were actually glued to the closed door. Better not to make a scene.

So there she is, packed into the crowded train. Duck bills stick out of baskets. She wanted to die. "And after I had given him everything!" It would make a perfect melodrama for the tabloids; you'd just need a little imagination to fill in the gaps, and everyone would be in tears. Too bad that we can't direct all our anger at Alexander, but he's simply mediocre, like the rest of us who reserve our courage for history, which gets its start and gathers speed from all our acts of cowardice.

She had to look for connections, make appointments, wait, start off again, come back, negotiate terms and guarantee payment, all in order to achieve a goal she despised. Finally, she is at the doctor's, rue Marcadet, this gentle soul still dreaming of being able to start again from square one, to become once more a woman whom Alexander would find acceptable. The doctor seems angry; he's only pretending, but how can she know that? "There's a difference," he was saying, "between a woman and an animal. A woman has a head to warn her about consequences." Didn't she know what a contraceptive is? "It will be fifty thousand francs." After all, he was doing her a favor.

She slammed the door in his face. In her scorn she regained her dignity. She preferred to be classed with the animals, since they did not refuse life. She was taking the side of the poor, faceless child, whom everyone rejected.

43

She didn't make her decision on the basis of morality, unless you mean that sometimes the moral law is the same as stubbornness, a rebellion in the name of life. Several times during the following nights, she had the same dream: she'd be running in the forest in order to get away from the child, but the child always reappeared in front of her and signaled to her. Her decision had been confirmed.

"What's the matter, mon peitit père?" she kept saying, as the tears flowed down his long face without his seeming to be aware of them.

For the first time she felt the heavens moving.

"I'm trying to understand," the man was saying. "Don't hold it against me. I didn't know to whom . . . . It must seem very odd to you. I had always thought that . . . ."

She was on her knees, towel in hand. She saw his long face from top to bottom, as in a movie shot — eyes slightly bulging, heavy eyelids — at the same time as her father was moving forward in the line. They gave him a towel and a bar of soap for this shower from which no one returned. A helmeted Nazi, machine gun at his chest, was handing her the towel and the soap . . . . There were little drops of sweat on the man's upper lip. She got up, went to dampen the worn, almost transparent towel, knelt down again and cooled his face. A white fluff of soapsuds was still in his beard; she wiped it away.

Did he even see her? His glance seemed to go through her. Then all at once he became another man and began to speak with dignity.

"In the whole world, there's no one in the whole world, Madame, who could have listened to me the way you have."

"Madame, you call me Madame? . . . . You just paid me for . . ." she said. "Besides, you haven't said anything."

"Is that really so?" he says, unbelieving.

"Who do you think I am? I'm not a Sister of Charity."

"Yes you are," he said, "yes you are. A Sister of Charity. And I had always thought . . . ."

Elizabeth had been wrong to be so worried. War was changing the order of things. The dishonor she had feared for her father and his pain were swept away in another shame, another pain. She no longer had anyone to confess to.

Her father had refused to wear the yellow star. One morning about eight o'clock, a helmeted German carrying a machine gun — the same one she had seen in that line in front of the crematorium, because for her there was only one German soldier in the world, the one who had slapped her father because he had not stood up fast enough — a helmeted German had appeared at their little apartment on the rue de Levis. Her father was sitting there, filling his pipe. He had just said, as he did so often, "Elizabeth, you touched the hands of the clock. Haven't I forbidden you to touch the clock?" It was an obsession: he had a passion for Louis XVI, Empire, and Restoration clocks. Elizabeth had thrown herself on her knees; the soldier had knocked her away with the barrel of his gun. Later, she found out: her father, who was always tired, who was afraid of everything and was upset if she dusted the clock, was making delayed-action bombs in the cellar. It was hard to understand. Those who are closest to us prefer to show us their familiar, reassuring face.

45

She had been wrong to be uneasy: her father would never know. She was alone with her child. Incomprehensibly, the executioners had ignored the two of them. As for the world, it dismissed them, attentive only to the sounds of war. It was pre-occupied with survival, and how to make a profit out of tragedy. Alexander, who was fighting on the Eastern front, was finding what he wanted . . . . Or had he run away just because of her and her baby? But what was really important? She had died at the same time as her father and her lover; she was dead to all sentiment and morality. She had turned her heart to stone; she had only one idea in her head: that she would save this child from everyone — her daughter, since it was a daughter. And because all doors were closed to her because she was Jewish, because she was a mother, she had taken up the profession, had become a woman without a face, without remembrance, without regret.

This threadbare towel with which she wiped the man's face to remove the sweat from his moustache — it was enough to make her suddenly remember how she had knelt in front of her father, wiping the blood flowing from his lips. And wiping the dab of soap from this man's beard was all that was needed to break down some inner barrier, allowing a strange sweetness to invade her spirit. In a flash she relives what had wounded her, but in a different way. How could someone have suffered so much, placed her feelings in limbo for such a long time, and then find herself alive again, her former soul restored, almost happy? It's as if happiness had always been intact, deep down inside; all that was needed was for something to burst forth. A happiness without hope, almost motionless, without explanation — it is always within us, but we usually reject it, caught up in our day-to-day affairs; all that is needed is a single distraction, a moment of self-forgetfulness.

We fall in love, build up hopes, get caught up in some enthusiasm; we suffer, fall into despair, believe that this or that is all-important. My life, what has happened to it? My lost happiness, the years that have fled by . . . . It hardly amounted to anything except for its secret interior meaning, an impression that is beyond time . . . like a word, a phrase, a touch, whose significance is beyond, but would not exist without that word or touch or brush stroke or wound. We believe in the inevitable; we make something external out of what is interior and indestructible, yet a moment of self-forgetfulness, a tiny crack in the surface, that's all it takes — such moments of grace are like one's native place, an island adrift.

That's why story-telling is different from reporting. You have to fill in the gaps with images and feelings in the same way people collect souvenirs, anecdotes to entertain tourists of the spirit who are hopelessly addicted to the picturesque and have an artificial belief in "special moments." The narrator has to run, leap, fly like a stream of lightning into a life, whether our own or that of our characters, from nothing before, from an infinity of before to an infinity of afterwards, to nothing afterwards, to the eternal afterwards, between birth and death, across islands of plenty where the infinite seems to break forth as in an asymptote, where the straight line can almost reach the curve, as if it were possible to reach a truth more real than the truth of images or even of ideas.

Everyday conversation is only an exchange of banal catch-phrases, buzz-words, until the moment when someone speaks from her own point of view, with her individual voice, and a feeling rises up from the depths, a revelation that is authentically personal. It's the same in books: everything is pointless if it is not the irrepressible flash of that most intimate truth which belongs to everybody . . . .

Our exile is bearable, surely, only because there exists this lost frontier which is rediscovered beyond everything that protects and masks it — words, bricks, wallpaper . . . . As if these impressions that can arise from a blend of commonplace memories and come unexpectedly, without warning, nudging us with a slight kick, scratching our hearts with a sharp pain, as if these impressions — alive in us, almost independent of us, and often unknown to us — prove to be the most intimate, most incommunicable and yet most universal part of us, if at least the word is spoken that will give them existence. It is not always necessary to have experienced them ourselves. All of us believe we can recognize them in the quivering of a voice or the immediacy of a passage of writing, and we share in the happiness of the one who gives voice to them, without perhaps having lived them, but because we have recognized them on a face. For what has been kept in the depth of one's being becomes also, for a second, this wrinkle of the forehead or these lips, as necessary, unexpected, and unforeseeable as traces that have been left on stone by rain, wind, and sea.

Such impressions are as true as abstract ideas — more so. We don't really know how to decipher those ideas and the words are given to us only in order that we may rediscover the throbbing of those moments which have been lost and found again, and are now fixed and immovable for the rest of our lives, the secret joy beyond time when eternity spills over. Perhaps the man himself, freed from his own anguish, had already read such signs on the young woman's face, and that is why he spoke to her so gravely, "Madame, no one in the whole world . . . ."

It was at that moment that she had felt the heavens move — and it was as astonishing as the first time she had felt her daughter stir in her womb — at the very moment she was wiping the lips of the man and brushing away the fluffy thread.

"It's all because of my daughter," the man said. "She left home and is wandering around Paris, and she . . . ."

Always had done the proper thing. Always dutiful, accountable. Married a young widow who already had a son — a noble act. She was a pious woman. Every Saturday he made his confession to the archpriest of the cathedral. But he had no luck with his children. It was unbelievable. There was something wrong in what people had always told him, in what he himself had believed. Bruno, his wife's son, disappeared without leaving a trace. You could put the blame on Paris or the young people he'd fallen in with. It hadn't done much good that he loved Bruno. He believed he loved him like a son, even though he wasn't his son. But Martine, his own daughter! He had married a saint, and he himself was a believer, a regular churchgoer, president of the parish council . . . . And now, this young woman . . . .

"And you," he asked, "are you a believer?

"Yes," she said. "I'm Jewish, but ever since I've been in this profession nothing has any importance any more; everything I'm doing is . . . ."

"No," the man said, again putting aside his own problem, "you've been misinformed. Whatever good that we do remains good even in the midst of evil. The important thing is not to think too highly of oneself. As for good and evil, there's almost nothing separating them, an abyss no thicker than cigarette paper."

"How do you know that?"

"It's what I've been taught. Some things stay with you without your even being aware of them."

"But I'm not a Christian."

"That doesn't make any difference. Ever since He is risen, everyone in the world is Christian. A woman like you, He would have asked you for a drink of water."

He seemed like someone bringing good news. He forgot to say what he intended to say and she forgot to ask him.

"You talk just like Strozzi," she said.

Images surfaced from deep waters, and slowly unfolded: the train, the bourgeois salon at Laval, Alexander's murderous look, the helmeted soldier with the machine-gun, the column of deportees. She carried all those images within her just as one lives with metal sounds without noticing them . . . . How is it possible to have suffered for so long, to have seen the traces of war disappear little by little along with hatred, and then have life, which had rejected you, begin to bubble up, and suddenly find yourself almost happy again? Twenty years washed away. I'd like to know how it can happen, and be able to describe it. It all takes place, however, without any words, without any speeches.

The man must have finally finished his explanation, since she stands up, gets dressed in a flash, grabs her coat, and pulls him along, as vivacious as before all her troubles . . . . I can see the man get up, find his way to the telephone, and then freeze. His instinctive reflexes are still with him. What was he going to tell his wife? The words were already formed in his head: "Madeleine, ask the children to say their prayers; I'm going to meet Martine."

Laure and Virginie, the two youngest children, who were still at home, were terribly pious. They took literally everything the priest said; they even kept a record of all their sacrifices. How long would all this continue? There was something about it that wasn't right. Their mother would have them kneel in front of the crucifix in the living room, and they would recite the rosary for poor Martine.

Five years ago Martine, along with her younger sisters, had prayed in the same way for poor Bruno, after he had finally picked up his son's trail . . . . For months he had been without any news of Bruno, though bills kept rolling in. Finally, he had taken the night train, arriving in Paris in the early morning. "Madeleine, ask the children to say their prayers; I'm going to meet Bruno." It was absurd; he had fainted in the bar where his son had arranged for them to meet.

"Look, sir, you're a good fellow but we have absolutely nothing in common. Home has the smell of the sacristy, all we hear about are principles . . . . My mother is still living with her first husband, my father; and you, you put up with everything — it's a little pathetic. Let me live my own life. Victims — that's what all of you are. I'm taking off day after tomorrow; my paper has given me an assignment in Tokyo."

"Good," the woman said, "let me call Strozzi. If Strozzi doesn't find her, no one can. Strozzi has a whole network of friends."

To see her walk, quick and lighthearted, would you guess that she's one of them? Perhaps. The heart can change in an instant; appearances fade away slowly. The man has forgotten his umbrella — that's touching, and a good sign. The umbrella stays in the room, hooked to the bedstead.

Pigalle bursts into the man's consciousness as they proceed down the street, almost running. Night falls. The city breathes excitement. The crowd comes and goes under the flood of lights, propelled by some external force. The individuals may change but the crowd remains the same, as unchanging as the fifteen-cent dreams, the continuous strip tease joints, the all-night movie theaters. In the middle of the street, pushed and pulled like the blood in one's arteries, the crowd bumps against the doors of bars like blood against the limits of the body. It is snatched up for a moment, then rejected, along with its desires and pleasures — jazz to make life dance, tender human flesh to enjoy, suffer, and die . . . .

When she first walked the streets, she made it a point of honor to wait for the client to approach her. Bon soir, merci. Others would seek out prospects for her, haggle over prices. When she accepted the client, her face was impenetrable, like Tamar in the Bible when she gave herself to Judah. (In the novel I had started, Tamar was what I was going to call Elizabeth.) In reality, she had received only one man; they were all the same but with different masks. There was nothing except her service, neither love nor friendship. Feelings were dead. She staked her honor on it, she was only an official functionary. When all was said and done, cloistered. Afterwards she would go home, to the rue de Levis, another world. For twenty years it went on. Was it really possible?

"On the Champs-Elysées, did you say? Yes, I know some girls there. My first ten years, I worked the avenue. It's a question of age. Don't be afraid, petit père, you're going to see Strozzi. He's really something. What in the world could you have done that your Martine would get an idea like that? She must be pig-headed . . . . Taxi!"

I would have spun out the story. How the banker waited in a bar until early morning. Thomas Postel, that was the banker's name. How Elizabeth and Strozzi found Martine. Nothing broken. Yes, she'd been thinking about leaving home ever since the evening she graduated . . . . She had drifted around for a few days in Paris. As soon as a man approached her in a bar and struck up a conversation, she ran away. It was more than she could handle. Even on the street, there was an air about her that frightened them off . . . .

"Corruption of a minor, do you know how long a sentence they hand out for that? When there's a young girl in that line of work, usually there's a pimp not far behind. You get a customer, and the guy arrives a minute later. 'One

52

hundred thousand francs, gramps, or we'll leak the whole affair.' It's easy to see you're not in the profession."

Martine began to cry. Hard to know if it was relief at having been found, or because she hadn't found a man by herself. Tonzi and Elizabeth listened to her story before they rejoined her father. By turns she was stubborn, brash, and timid . . . . Any mention of morality made her think of her father, how his beard scratched when she had to embrace him, especially the odor of his mouth, the putrid tobacco smell . . . .

"Every Sunday after vespers, we all went to the cemetery to pray at the family tomb. Yes, we really did; it's perfectly true." All their expenses were entered in a little black notebook with red lines dividing the pages into columns: "Tea for Laura and Virginie, a permanent for Martine" . . . . She'd be having a great time listening to a record; her mother would come in, Martine would get stiff as a pole, and couldn't hear the rest of the music. "Yes, they were always ready to forgive, that was true, but their forgiveness was another blow. They probably made an entry of that, too, in the little black notebook" . . . . There were too many boys in Rouen buzzing around her, who wanted only one thing. So she might as well take the initiative . . . . She was mixing everything up.

"You're imagining things, Martine," Strozzi had said. "Boys try their luck in Rouen like everywhere else."

They finally learned what touched off her decision to leave home. It was the Red Cross dance, a ball for debutantes. Every year forty daughters from the best families, all dressed up in the latest styles, were presented in the ballroom of the City Hall. It was quite a show. All the society big-wigs without exception were there, parents dressed in their finest, teary-eyed, like at a First Communion. Her mother, who was president of some association, had encouraged her. At first Martine didn't want any part of it because . . . but then the idea of a new formal and the dance won her over.

Actually, Martine didn't have the temperament for this sort of thing; that was evident right away. She was rather listless, a painted china doll.

As they were leaving that evening, a young man advanced through the sea of white bouffant skirts and slapped her roundly . . . . Yes, of course, she loved him. Besides, this wild young man had warned her: "The worst prostitution," he had said, "is the kind that doesn't own up to it. I'd rather see you in a bikini in a beauty contest — it would be more honest. I could never marry a debutante, some dressed-up doll." The very next day she had taken the train to Paris . . . . A perfect melodrama.

Later, they were all in a restaurant at Les Halles, the father with his lost sheep. ("Let's go to Les Halles for some onion soup," Strozzi suggested, "we'll have a chance to talk.")

"I like that boy of Martine's," Strozzi had declared. "He's my kind, just like your son Bruno."

Thomas Postel raised his eyes, looking like a frightened fish. A sly smile lit up Martine's teary eyes. No, there was nothing very remarkable about her — just a flighty, pretty girl. All she was capable of was one small explosion.

I would have spun out the melodrama. There was a drunken American from Arizona who attached himself to Elizabeth and Martine. "I'm lost here," he was saying, "my mother died in Arizona. All that I've got left are dollars. Tell me that you love me." The American was completely blotto — no pain could reach him.

"Tell him what he wants, sing it to him," Strozzi said to Elizabeth and Martine. "Come over here, pal," he said to the American; "have some soup with us.

The American kept repeating, "Tell me something, tell me something. Once more, once more." He began to spill out his whole life story. Strozzi was laughing at it all, while Thomas Postel looked on, bewildered, dazed, and incredulous.

"Could I see you again?" Thomas Postel had asked. He was like a school kid, shy but fascinated, who stays after school because he didn't understand everything. Amazing, some of the things Tonzi had said. Like: "Principles never saved anyone. All that parents can really do for their children is surround them with the warmth of love. What's necessary is to be alive, and to live at a certain height. Don't put so much emphasis on duty; better not to be too conscious of it when you're doing your duty. Has there ever been a child conceived out of duty? Poor kid! It's a good thing that sons and daughters rebel against their fine respectable families, who are all too often bound by dead loyalties." This was strange advice, a whole new world. Strozzi had blown up all of Thomas Postel's received ideas.

I would have liked to pursue the story of Martine and her banker father. What would become of her? The superficial rebellions of young people are often followed by the worst compromises. As for Thomas Postel de Séverac, born plain Postel, I thought I could figure him out. Forgetting prudence, ignoring his archpriest, he had the absurd idea of going to see a....in order to understand, to ask for help. Was he ever going to break free and begin to live? And if he did, what would become of the false peace of his home?

The banker was accustomed to playing the role of family counselor — the heart and loins of the strong box, its very soul — an attentive, perhaps overly attentive spouse, a father who knew his responsibilities. It would be monstrous to question his motives, to doubt his good intentions. Nevertheless, projecting his fear and his boredom onto his own family gave him a subtle pleasure; there was a refined, comfortable self-satisfaction in defending goodness, truth, and order.

Out of love for him I would have been pitiless. Is there any point in having firewood if there's nothing to light it? Why have well-marked boundaries if there is no road? What is life if there is no joy? All those prejudices, proprieties, and social conventions were a denial of joy. I would have stripped off the mask that had become glued to his skin. The armor of dignity was denying him the dignity of being a man. Thomas would discover that he had never loved, that he had forced himself, given in to necessity. Can a love born of duty be really love?

But Thomas would wake up. I think that one day he'll actually hear his wife's voice — for the first time . . . .

That voice reflected fairly accurately the emptiness of a mind, the barren waste of a soul. It was a monotonous voice, without warmth, terribly lonely. It would have been better if the cord, which was stretched too tightly, would snap. Let yourself live a little, Madeleine; forget all those pious clichés.

"Madame Dupont confided in me today. Their marriage is going through real difficulty. Let's include their intentions in our prayers, Thomas."

Or: "Madame Dupont is in a bad way. She no longer talks about her marital problems; it's clear to me that she's becoming bitter." It never occurred to her that Madame Dupont might have sensed the phoniness of Madeleine's "religious" interest.

Or perhaps: "Monsieur Guillot has finally decided to get involved in apostolic work. You ought to go over his financial affairs with him; it might encourage him to persevere. God makes use of humble things."

Formerly, he would have listened to all that; he would even have tried to admire it. "My wife is a saint," he would say. He used to try to raise himself to her heights.

Separate rooms, they'd slept in separate rooms for a long time. The purpose of love was only to produce children — that was church doctrine. At least that's what Madeleine de Séverac said, a militant Catholic, president of the women's guild. With what zeal Thomas had lent himself to that sacrifice! That's what gave him the appearance of a fish whose scales were peeling.

Saturday evenings, before God, he dutifully examined his conduct. Before what God? The archpriest received him in his office. When Thomas accused himself of bad thoughts, the archpriest tapped him on the shoulder, and told him to say one Our Father and one Hail Mary, but was careful not to bring up the real questions. But how could he? He'd never asked them of himself.

That was what had given Thomas Postel self-assurance — the self-assurance of a wood-louse. Would he continue to see the archpriest on Saturday evenings? Otherwise, he would have to lie, because Madeleine would ask, before they sat down for dinner, "Thomas dear, did you stop at the cathedral this evening? How is our dear, dear Monsignor?"

Women who so easily solve their personal problems often give free rein to their will to power under the flattering mask of religious or ethical activity. They are frightening, all the more so because some ministers of religion easily become their dupes. The worldly station of these women permits their idle concerns to become installed at the periphery of life. If they happen to meet resistance, their escape is God. They promise to pray for their critics, pardoning those who ask neither for their prayers nor their pardon. They proclaim their devotion, their undying attachment to the church, and are always prepared to quote passages from the Councils. They're actually sincere but their truth is counterfeit.

Madeleine fit into pious phrases like fingers in a glove. She sweetly gathered up the troubles of others in order to draw a lesson from them. Her moralizing went on endlessly, making everything clear, dull, and meaningless. She would quote a bishop here, or St. Paul there; it served to shut you up. She was as versed in theology as a nanny goat in electronics. She had swallowed key phrases from clerical magazines and attended conferences on "The church in crisis." Her mind spun around from one thing to another.

The important thing was not to recognize one's own poverty, to forget the pain of one's own emptiness. Women like that turn you against morality; they make it clear that spiritual prostitution is the worst kind. She adopts attitudes, makes use of the right phrases, but every pore of her being tells you that all this effort is meaningless . . . I found no special trait in Madeleine de Séverac, no individual approach. I had met her before, under ten, twenty, a hundred faces, both male and female.

But the novelist is fair: he describes, he doesn't judge. His harshness is a kind of testimony of his love. Was it her fault that she had lost her first husband in World War I? She had remarried because of a sense of duty to her son, had insisted on keeping her name. Thomas Postel, for his part, had been very happy to marry a name. When you get to the bottom of things, you always find someone who has been hurt. The same kind of pain that had led Elizabeth to her profession was responsible for Madeleine's unhappy home where her children were dying from the cold. Yes, she was faithful — faithful, without even knowing it, to her first husband — but there was no one to point it out to her. Like everyone else, she had protected herself; she was no better, no worse.

I think that I would have pitied her. Too bright a light would have killed Madeleine. Maybe Thomas would have been capable of loving her, accepting the painful reality of her personality. He might well be willing to put up with her habit of thinking in circles. Was this because he lacked courage? Or was such a response genuine charity? As if feelings could exist in a pure state! More simply, he would probably have become an accomplice of his daughters. I can see them exchanging glances around the table, while Madeleine remained oblivious to what was going on. He would manage to hand out a few permissions. Thomas Postel would become rather skeptical about his old formulas, and begin to go to the movies. No more little black books with red lines. He would go to Paris more often; Madeleine would accuse him of spending time in bad company. In fact, he'd be going to Paris to see Strozzi. But she would think he was being unfaithful, deceiving her, and would offer up her suffering for the salvation of both her husbands. But I'm much too fascinated with Jerome Strozzi to stay in Rouen any longer. Exit Thomas. Exit Madeleine. Exit Martine. That's the end of their story!

The meeting of Elizabeth, Thomas, and Martine, on that wild night when Strozzi located that young woman, had been decisive. A few weeks later, Elizabeth left Paris for Taussat. When I asked her how this dull banker from Rouen could have had such an influence on her, at first she just said, "It was because of images that came to me. I began to feel ill." Everything had begun again through sadness: when she had seen Alexander, and then her father, exactly as if the events had just taken place, that very instant. The hurt and the pain had begun to cut the threads of countless sutures, as if memory were more in her body than in her head.

A little later, however, she said that for several months she had felt something was going to happen. To be precise, it was since she had met Jerome Strozzi. She'd heard the other girls talk about him. They teased him, they laughed at him but, no doubt out of a sense of modesty, in a kindly way. Somehow, he seemed to give them the courage to go on living and sometimes he helped straighten out their affairs.

So Elizabeth had phoned Strozzi. Clarissa, her daughter, was now a college student, and on no account did she want her to find out about her mother. Lying was beginning to be more and more difficult. Strozzi had come to their two-room apartment on the rue de Levis, since she had always succeeded in keeping her profession separate from her personal life. Jerome immediately found a way to deal with her problem. He knew a great many people, even some professors at the Sorbonne. Everything was arranged in two weeks: Clarissa would get a scholarship to Cambridge. As early as the second visit, even though he hadn't asked her anything, for the first time in twenty years, Elizabeth talked freely and told him the whole story. Incredible.

"From the first time I saw him," she was saying, "I had a feeling that something — I didn't know what — was going to happen."

"Sure," I laughed, "lots of people have premonitions. One out of ten thousand times, something does happen. For example, every time a person gets in his car, he thinks about a possible accident. When it finally takes place, he says, 'I had a premonition.'"

"No, it's not that. I was sure of something . . . . It was a kind of calm happiness, the feeling of being loved, can you understand? Why are you looking at me like that? Your eyes seem to bore into me — do you think I'm . . . . ?"

"Well, what did he say? What did he do?"

"Nothing. He just came in and sat down. I was mending or reading. Oh no, one of the first times he came, he tried to make me angry. I had told him never to speak to me again about Alexander. Suddenly he blurted out, 'I think I'd have liked Alexander.' Or perhaps, 'Alexander wasn't just anyone; he was someone special.' Finally I got up, opened the door, and told him to get out. He said, 'I wanted to see your eyes flash, I want to bring you back to life. Your eyes were dead, Elizabeth. Now your eyes are coming alive; a new life is going to begin.'"

"My life," she said. "Strozzi kept saying that a life consisted primarily in what was still ahead of you. The past hardly mattered. 'What difference does it make,' he said, 'that someone's been this or that? What counts is from now on. Arise, take up . . . .' Then he stopped short and apologized."

And I tried to imagine him, this old man whom I hadn't yet seen, who suddenly stopped talking because he'd caught himself quoting the Gospel and didn't like to use its words as weapons. A long time ago he had recognized as a secret vice the habit of embracing formulas, building arguments, using the Son of Man as another object, situating Jesus in history instead of, even today, living one's life sufficiently within His so as to grasp the meaning of those phrases, and trying over and over to understand them. He apologized for being tactless, because it seemed to him that no one had the right to use these words if his own life had not first transformed them into bread and wine, into flesh and blood, and if he couldn't say them in his own personal voice.

"'Elizabeth, we invent the past here, in our head. It becomes hard as stone, my dear'" — yes, he often called her 'my dear.'

"'We haven't begun to plumb the depths of our freedom,' he said. 'Nothing has happened except what we wanted to happen, which continues to happen even today. Hardly anyone is willing to take this into consideration. Because we're afraid of dying, we avoid life, pass it by.'

"When two persons love one another, whether they know it or are still unaware of their love, they are simply there, silent, bathed in its warmth. Nothing is the same any longer — not even the quality of the air, or the sounds around them. Even inanimate objects are friendly. This condition usually doesn't last very long; it's something special. All the poetry of the world converges in this experience and explodes in vertigo; then it dissolves, and the world grows hard again."

Elizabeth could find no other way to explain Strozzi than to speak of his voice. "It seemed to have crossed deserts," she said, "knocked over countless walls. Seemed to emerge from an experience that was different from ordinary life. It's as if he were making love to you without his realizing it — and without your realizing it, either. But it lasts. You feel like forgiving everyone

61

that ever hurt you. You'd like to pour out on others the love that he has given you .... I think that's why I helped Thomas Postel and Martine. When I think that I am loved by a .... "

"What sort of love, Elizabeth?"

"It wasn't any kind I'd known .... He loved everyone with the same love," she said. "The love of God — whatever that meant for him." As for herself, she had never seen God, and as far as the church was concerned .... She thought of priests as a group — they had no individual faces, they were like ticket-takers at the train station.

"I'm beginning to believe everything that Strozzi believes," Elizabeth went on. "He says he never has a meal without thinking of the Last Supper. Do you know how he ends his letters? 'Je t'aime.' I love you. That's Strozzi. No way to be mistaken. I knew what he meant."

I wanted to tell this incredible story of Elizabeth at Taussat, after she found that her heart was still intact after twenty years. But I was wrapped up in my work, my way of seeing things, the pine trees and the sea. On one side there was the dreariness of the inlet, which empties itself and then refills, the smell of algae, and miles of paths through the pines, whose branches are like arms that arise from our own depths; then, having crossed the wooded dunes, there is the African coast stretching away in the distance. This flat inlet, with the vertical lines of the pines, the steeple of the village church, the perpendicular line of the coast beyond the dunes — it seemed to me that it all constituted a direct, austere language in which there was no longer a place for individual details, because objects that have been there in harmony with each other there for centuries call us to patience and freedom of spirit in the midst of this world's adversity. Brought back to life, Elizabeth's thoughts were scarcely thoughts; they sprang equally from the trees and the sea: "You are only one little wave. Let yourself do and undo things, but sing out of your own liberty."

I'd have liked to summon up Elizabeth's recollections as she slowly recast a new memory for herself. Her soul had been frozen and placed in hibernation; now she was rediscovering unique impressions, impossible to repress, beyond time. I'd have made her a sister to those women who have become famous because they fought to wrench every fleeting, passing feature from their love, as if they feared an ephemeral object that was too precisely formed, and wanted to expand their heart indefinitely.

Now everything was unfolding in a different light. Elizabeth is the one who had burdened Alexander with her impatient love. Alexander did not want to be loved. She had dreamed him into being, constructed him, and judged him, instead of seeing him as he really was. She had seen only calculation and flight in his ideas about pleasure. In fact, it was simply his extreme modesty. With the passing of years she heard his voice better, a voice that spoke about death. It didn't matter that he hadn't always been faithful to that voice. After all, who was faithful? It was a voice that came from far away, from a point in the depths of everyone — the call to disappear in order to leave room. Old images returned to her, taking on new meaning. How many times, looking at him when his eyes were closed, had she known that he would never be her husband? "I must hold on to this image," she told herself, "so that I can find it again when everything will be over." And yet she had persisted in fashioning him according to her own laws, her own desires. His murmur of "Je t'aime", "I love you," had only been the sigh of the flesh.

The first time she had said to him, "Je t'aime," he had become pale and said, "Be quiet. Wait a little — a day, ten days, a thousand. Such a phrase should only be spoken once in a lifetime." She had looked at him. A tear was falling from his closed eyes. She had taken his hand, but he brusquely pushed it away: "Don't touch me. I'm not the one you should look at. We can only meet in the music, far away. It's taken years to understand Bach or the meaning of Mozart."

Or that evening when they had stretched out under the pine trees and she had seen a falling star: "May Alexander always love me," she had wished. She had scarcely formulated the wish when a glow worm fell in her hair. She took it for a sign that her wish had been granted, and a great happiness came over her.

And what had Alexander said? That wishes like that were absurd. "Each of us has to be his own good luck."

She quoted a poet — she didn't know his name, but the words had been forever engraved on her mind and heart:

> *To be loved is to disappear*
> *To love is to shine with a never-failing light.*
> *To be loved is to disappear.*
> *To love is to endure.*

She hadn't formulated her request very well but she had seen, nevertheless, that her wish had been granted, since she loved forever. By now Alexander might be no more than some whitened bones in the Ukraine; she loved him with that expanded love that makes the one who loves go on existing. I would have been tempted to try to fix Elizabeth's happiness in words, like a little cloud that was beyond the cross currents of the wind. Had she previously been a victim of illusion, or was she now? What did it matter? At least she was not dreaming her new life. Her joy was a reality that contained its own proof, since she radiated joy all around her. I could have followed her in her little gray car on her trips around the village. Like Strozzi, she used to drop in on people, try to lend a hand. But how does one describe a charity as discreet, unobtrusive, and unaffected as this without turning it into a catechism lesson, without making it either pretentious or superficial?

In winter she'd go into the forest to get firewood. The practice here must have remained as it was in the old days: you had to get permission from the Mayor. It wasn't always easy to make both ends meet; everything she had went to support Clarissa. After all, few people make a fortune in the life.

But Jerome Strozzi had made that story pointless. As soon as I met him in Paris, I knew that he was the only one I could speak about. I had been looking for the source, the key. Now I had found Strozzi.

Strozzi with his gray-blue eyes, the blue of a thunderbolt. No, I made that up. Actually, it never occurred to me to look at the color of his eyes. Writing is an odd business — you don't really see anything; the pen or the typewriter does your seeing for you. The tempest in his eyes no longer flashes out, that purple flame which would blaze in his left eye when he was angry. Because something happened.

He had a stunned look in his eyes, but he was profoundly attentive to what was going on. Though there was not a hair on his head, an inner joy was reflected on his long face — just the opposite of that famous Christian hack writer who so impressed us when I was young. Strozzi had the profile and the look of an eagle who watches something intently, outside and within. His wit would flash out, a pithy phrase would emerge; it was the song of someone who had been hurt. Exultation as well as regret are engraved on this distinguished mask that is never at rest, bathed in an aureole of pride and humility. Probably best to think of the face of that old atheist-mystic Henry Miller, shining with a certain peace, or like one of those Indian gurus, a face of light bronze. That's Tonzi — as soon as he closed his eyes, you got a hint of the majesty of death.

If he wore a white collar and tie, and had a suitcase or an umbrella in his hand, you'd take him for a retired banker or lawyer. With his dark jacket, bottle-green polo shirt, Basque beret, he might be an elderly craftsman, or a pimp who's done time and, out of habit, still walks the streets of Clichy,

Pigalle, like an old sailor who never leaves the harbor. He resembles Brice, especially his eyes, I'm not sure exactly how. He has hardly any confidence in words. A preference and gift for friendship. A thoroughbred.

I've met people like him everywhere — rebels, some would call them, but they're not rebels in the name of ideas or theories. It's just that one day freedom takes hold of them and turns them upside down, and suddenly they're fighting against all kinds of unquestioned social assumptions. They are the ones who are really faithful. Faithful to what? To the law of their very nature, perhaps a grace. Are they anarchists? No. They do what is necessary. To Caesar the things that are Caesar's, and then goodbye. How do they handle their affairs? They do about as well in business as anyone else. It isn't so difficult to succeed; what's hard is setting limits on one's success. The point is that a day comes when their possessions become tiresome, and their hands open . . . . They're capable of serving a cause. But once the cause triumphs, they turn against it in the name of the same urgency that made them take it up in the first place. Clever with words, convincing speakers, they could easily be successful as communication specialists. But no, they'd rather leave those things to the sophists. The kind of people I'm speaking of deliberately don't employ all their weapons.

Perhaps a secret path leads them toward martyrdom. Not that they hold a grudge against society. They find society loveless, but prefer to bless it for tolerating them, and for giving them the opportunity, using the very structures it creates, to build up societies of true friends. When you meet them, it's like having your guide at the site of a volcano suddenly stop, lean over, and say, "Touch that right here; see — it's warm." And you lean over, the fire is burning underneath; you light a cigarette, and you can see those holes in the volcano that let the fire escape. Rebels prove the presence of fire.

If you're in a bar in Madrid, a spot like the Gran Via, for example, watching the customers and how they're dressed, every time a certain kind of man comes in you say to yourself, "There's the boss." It's just the way he has of greeting the others, the bartender and some of the regulars, with a dignified but familiar, protective air, and of leaning on the counter of the bar, next to the young woman at the cashier's desk, his left hand closed on the lining of his jacket, his right placed flat against his hip. It's the way he turns his head ever so slightly, glancing at the clientele like a *maître d*, then leaning toward the cashier with a concerned, business-like look. You say to yourself, "That's the boss." And when a newcomer come in, the whole scenario is repeated. It's a tic, it's in their blood; it shows in the small of the back, straightens them up right to the nape of their neck, and gives them the air of being perfectly at home anywhere in the world. There was nothing special about Strozzi's appearance: you might take him for anyone; you might elbow past him at the bar or even give him a shove. His dignity derives from something farther away.

To think that you might meet Strozzi on the sidewalks of the eighteenth arrondissement and take him for a retired . . . . It's the same with the Son of man. Since the death of the last disciple, no one can recall his face. Yet his face is everywhere now--in the subway, at Pigalle, in Pekin, loved, betrayed, sent back to Pilate or Herod or Caiphas. How wonderful it was that day near the pool when he tells the paralytic to stand up. The people want to carry him off in triumph but he manages to get lost in the crowd. No one recognizes him. Even on our world's first morning Magdalen takes him for a gardener.

It's possible to rub shoulders with Strozzi, or even give him a shove. But once you start talking to him, and he speaks to you or you exchange glances, the silence glows; his look goes straight to your heart, and the vigor of life streams once again from his words. You stand up straighter; you no longer want to lie. Unhappiness is no longer the same unhappiness.

I've found someone to whom I could go to confession with my eyes wide open. Yes, I know, I can confess my sins in the dark, through the grille, a strainer through which both good and evil can pass. After all, it doesn't matter whether the confessor is scholarly, intelligent or stupid, good or evil — it can be anyone who will do the job correctly. I know what a sacrament means, that God does not lie, that he has bound himself to the actions of men, always available, like air, fire, or water. And if someone were eager enough, wasn't afraid of losing everything, wasn't too concerned about getting repaid in the afterlife for what he's giving up here and now — why, he could tell it all to his horse or his dog. He wouldn't even have to say anything, just a blink of the eyelids, a heartbeat, would be enough to turn life upside down and cause Jerusalem to arise.

It's crazy, but when I'm near Strozzi, I feel like saying Father. Frankly, I've never felt like saying that to anyone except during church services. Those people who use the word all the time give me a pain — they're like vendors shouting their wares on the street. But now I feel like saying Father. Strozzi hasn't been called that for a long time. It's odd: he had to give up the clerical uniform and official habits, and forget all the stock phrases of a priest so that an aura of fatherly compassion might spread over his face.

Old buddy, night-bird, with you and a few friends — including me, so I could tell the story — we might start some kind of a club. We'd have a badge so that we could recognize each other, something very small. No, we mustn't even have that. Soon there'd be mutual congratulations, we'd end up decorating each other. You tell people I'm great and I'll say the same about you. No, let the little flock remain scattered. Rebels are loners.

We all like to pigeonhole things, hand out labels. It's reassuring. Is Tonzi a good priest or a bad priest? Is he crazy or a saint? I have no idea. All I know is that as soon as someone discovers one small truth, and stands up for it, suddenly that person is all alone. *Sleep now, and take your rest.* The disciples *have to* sleep during that night of agony. It's *necessary* for Christians to sleep while countless sons of man pass by on the cross of life. It was thanks to an old man that Strozzi was able to go his own way freely. Yes, there was an old cardinal in Paris, lost in routine, who had awakened one day without warning.

Those impetuous reformers who would like to set an age limit for retirement make me laugh. Are these militants for Christendom so tired of waiting? They're in a rush to organize everything on the same principles as the big public bureaucracies, as if holy mother church wasn't already sick with too much administration! Why not set up Social Security, promotions based on age, honorary titles, an automatic medal after so many years, the whole works?

71

But if there's one thing I've noticed, it's that there are some doleful old men (it doesn't matter whether they're fat or skinny)who may have been elected, at a time when others had become fossilized, because they were considered safe and reliable, who hardly have taken the reins in their hands than they suddenly realize that they no longer have anything to lose. Backed up against the wall that is death, every kind of fear vanishes. They have drunk their cup of fatigue, and suddenly, visited by the Holy Spirit, look at them: firm, steady, incredibly young. And what strikes me is precisely this: the psychology championed by the new technicians of convert-making, trained for efficiency, armed with statistics and fired with ambition, is already out-dated and futile. It's not the wisdom of the aged that one should admire but the breath of madness which sometimes blows through them — as if reason has to be humbled, as if the Spirit could act only through weak instruments.

For example, a likeable old man, faintly skeptical, who has no general ideas, gets pushed onto the pontifical throne almost in spite of himself. All that's needed is a little prompting from the sidelines and you see him come on stage. "We can be relaxed and calm with him in this job, we know him," the top officials were saying; "he's never caused any trouble." And the rest of us, standing below, the rank and file who have no power, were saying to each other: "Hurrah, for once we're not going to have a distinguished pope, someone who's an orator and can speak a dozen languages. No more mythology; let's do without the prestige of a super-leader." The intellectuals, however, weren't happy, the Ph.D.'s who write learned articles in the reviews, clarify theological developments, and offer subtle observations. They thought he wasn't really the right type for such a prestigious office, but fortunately, at his age, the situation wouldn't last too long. Of course, six months later they had completely changed their attitude; they always follow the current opinion. They had to keep up with their followers, who are the real advance scouts. Suddenly there was a flood of proclamations, major articles, conferences, and pamphlets, all properly footnoted. It was a miracle, they said — adding that, of course, they had said as much all along.

Scarcely had he been elevated to the highest office in the church than the good old fellow comes down among the people, speaking a completely unpretentious language, without fear or anxiety, indifferent to appearances, free and unadorned. He speaks the one language everyone understands, the language of brotherhood, like that spoken by the disciples the morning of Pentecost. He didn't really need to speak at all. His eyes speak, his look, the very pores of his skin. This man actually speaks to men and women everywhere because he participates in the great common basis of humanity — which is stronger than all the copes and decorations and holy gold trimmings. He laughs, a laugh that cracks mirrors. He tells jokes that go the rounds. Like one about not taking himself for the pope. There's no claim of rights, no lessons to hand out, no lectures on morals. He exists; he himself is proof that faith goes to the very heart of life. All the others stand around in their armor, with their key ideas, their principles, and their sense of panic, just like the rich young man who refuses to let go of his wealth.

Now, at that time, many years before Rome felt the freshness of a new spring, the Holy Spirit was in Paris working on an elderly cardinal who suddenly became young again. There was a sparkle of youth at the residence of the nuncio, avenue Barbet-de-Jouy. It was marvelous and unexpected, almost scary. The old mansion trembled on its foundation. It no longer received only counts, knights of St. Gregory, society ladies who run charity drives, retired generals, and members of the Academy who had sold their soul to God — the flower of society but also humble curates from the poorest

73

parishes, ordinary workers, and trouble-making Dominicans. People were actually reading a pastoral letter issued by the cardinal, and a book called *France: Mission Country?* had just been published. Its author, Abbé Godin, had found a recruit, previously pursued by the Gestapo, just right for his research team. Yes, Tonzi was involved with them, sharing their new-found hope . . . .

The elderly archbishop gave them the green light: the team could operate independently, outside the official parish structures. France might well be mission country, but that didn't mean treating the French as barbarians and sending them bearded missionaries. Beards no longer impressed people. To educate, "to give people a formation," as they used to say, to provide a kind of conditioning — Godin's team believed there were better things to do. Enough of such schooling, they said. Leave the ceremonies to others, along with the glamor, the rhetoric, the archaeological bric-a-brac, the logical tricks that establish "truth," and the fake angels.

To be, that was what was needed. To stimulate people, spur them on, knowing that everything comes from within, that it's more important to be than to do. To stop lying in good faith; to recognize that we live in the diaspora and let the church finally become what it is, without those top-heavy, golden decorations. No more organizing appearances, frightening the poor, driving away men and women who have an instinct for freedom, and colonizing the world. Instead, let it be small and humble, the better to raise up the leaven, because it is the few who save, who prevent corruption. In short, the fundamental logic of the group was to remake the system, to repair each crack of history: to leave law, necessity, and folklore behind in order to be free; to prove life by living it. For what kind of faith is it that doesn't enter into life like an axe into wood, that no longer turns the world upside down but is hemmed in by the prejudices of class and country and the immense weight of its own wisdom?

There was, of course, opposition to their approach. This was normal, since it is necessary for the disciples to take their sleep in order that the Redemption may be accomplished. Many people prefer to stand on their dignity and hand down certitudes from above; all one then has to do is to blame everything on the times or on the Evil One. Underneath their uniforms they felt afraid; they dreaded the strong wind of ideas. It was a lot easier to say "Let us pray" or "Dominus vobiscum."

The team had decided to start off January 16, 1944. Godin looked at Strozzi and asked, "And what are we going to do with you?" But he already knew the answer. Since his meeting with Pâquerette and Sabine, Strozzi had penetrated the milieu of Pigalle, unintentionally, and quite naturally. The number of his parishioners, men and women without a parish, kept growing..

"No one else can be what you are," Godin says, "go to it."

That was how Strozzi was given his mission . . . . He didn't give it to himself. That's reassuring. It reassures him, too. Until 1953, although not officially connected with any parish or official group, he will continue to live in the little community of Saint Denis-La Chapelle. He's happy there, has friends in the group. After plunging into the nighttime world of unhappiness, it's good to have a snug place to come back to. No longer had a formal ministry. He was tired of theorists, had become more and more amazed that people could understand each other by using words. Words made miserable clacking sounds, like pistol shots at a shooting gallery. But at the house on the rue des Roses what he receives and what he gives is friendship, an irreplaceable gift. And it endures, incredible. Tonzi doesn't go back on his word to a friend. But the time comes when he is considered a dead weight on the parish. And for him the rectory is just a hotel-restaurant. His schedule is crazy, and they consider his clientele questionable. He disagrees. Some say that what he's doing is a sin. Strange that they hadn't noticed anything before. But to the degree that Godin's project might be called into question, the provincial begins to be afraid. Few men are willing to decide an issue in terms of the real weight of things. Truth reaches them only when it becomes a force. They don't want to admit that truth can be abandoned, solitary. They wait until a great many arrive on the scene to bless it, as if truth needed the support of large numbers; then they hurry forward to share in the victory.

Those among whom Tonzi operates represent a kind of underground, men and women of no account; for some such a work is evil and shouldn't exist — it would be best not to think about people like that. The conflict gets worse.

"They supported me for almost ten years; I'm very grateful for that. During the time when I was in authority at the seminary, suppose I had to deal with an individual like myself; what would I have done?"

Strozzi in the metro. Summoned to the archbishop's office for eight o'clock. That's no time for an appointment. Night is the time when Strozzi is active because night doesn't belong to the devil. That is when there are so many calls for help from desperate people, possible suicides. That's when there are so many nets spread out and one has to rescue victims who are too weak to avoid them, because we must never stop fighting for life against death.

Rue Barbet-de-Jouy — embassy row. He is received first by the chancellor of the archdiocese — what kind of a title is that? The mansion has long had a reputation for diplomacy, and those assigned there have common sense.

The chancellor would like it if Strozzi would simply leave Paris . . . . Moreover, they have nothing to reproach him for, as a man or a priest.

"Then what's it all about?"

The chancellor is accustomed to deal with frightened, apprehensive priests, not a sixty-year-old who asks for explicit reasons. His says His Eminence has received reports. His look is evasive.

The Archbishop greets Strozzi in a fatherly manner. But in spite of his benevolence the Archbishop is accustomed, after all, to moving in the best circles. He has connections with high society in Paris and Geneva. Why reproach him for that? He only followed his career. How could he see the real world except through the reports people gave him?

He's on his guard, perhaps protecting himself.

"I'm concerned about your health, my son, both physical and moral. When someone has led the kind of life you've been leading, there comes a time when one should begin to take it easy."

"Look at me," Strozzi says, "do I look like I don't have good physical and moral health?"

The Archbishop is plump and friendly. I can almost see the purple reflected on his chubby face, the amethyst on his finger as it taps lightly on the desk. In front of him there is Tonzi's bronzed face on the body of a boxer, and that luminous look that is totally without fear.

"But after all, the promiscuity, all those . . . . "

"They protect me, your Eminence, those . . . . They are women, your Eminence, human beings, creatures of God; the Son of God asked one of them for a drink. Your priests with their Children of Mary, the ladies who run charity benefits — you know better than I all the things that can be hidden under the cloak of piety. But are their sentimental illusions a sufficient reason to call their works into question? In my case, one ambiguous step, perhaps simply by a word or an indication of preference, and I'm finished.

The field of my ministry is infinitely more severe on me than any parish would be. How can I explain it to you? No one can understand it."

"But is it true that you embrace them?"

Strozzi suddenly found himself back in that dark room at the school at Thonon fifty years earlier. It was hardly worth the trouble of having grown up.

"Yes, on the forehead. Some of them, for a joke, pretend to kiss me on the lips. They need friendship. Sometimes one or another of them needs to cry and puts her head on my shoulder. Often they have neither father nor mother . . . . "

"Well, there are reports against you," the Archbishop says.

"What reports?" Tonzi asks.

"Ask the chancellor for them."

I can see that vein on Strozzi's right temple beginning to tremble as his powerful hands grasp the arms of his chair. "Who is lying here?" Strozzi asks. "The chancellor just told me . . . . "

You're naive, Tonzi. You know very well that lying is often called prudence. You're wasting your time by going on talking: "Who would you expect to make reports in my favor? Summon here those who have signed those reports; I believe I can explain them." You're naive, Tonzi.

"I live among those forsaken by society. They don't know your address. They don't even know you exist. They'd never think of turning in reports about anyone, like so many respectable people do . . . . ."

The intelligent glance of the Cardinal hesitates between anger and admiration. Who is this Strozzi? A saint, an eccentric, a poor wretch who needs the scum of society to help him breathe easily, a prophet? "If I had a whole crowd like him — but what can I do with just one?" The Cardinal neither judges nor condemns. He would like to continue peacefully on his path, and arrange everything smoothly.

"My son, I fear you want to put new wine into old bottles."
And so he sent Strozzi to his provincial superior.

And the latter one day hides behind economic reasons, withholds payment for Strozzi's food and lodging, asks him to return the key to the rectory, and gives him his priestly blessing.

Tonzi out on the street. Must have been sixty-three or sixty-five, something like that. It's one o'clock in the afternoon. The street is empty. It was bound to happen.

The pitcher goes so often to the well
It comes a-cropper at the end of the ditch.
We'd said as much all along.
God, they always say the same old thing, all the world over.

So Tonzi is out there on the street, carrying that same little suitcase with the square corners. But there's joy in his heart--let me tell you why. His order didn't place him under obedience. They just let him go, that's all — freedom. Therefore, he is still a priest of the Catholic, apostolic, and Roman church.

Friends found him a place to stay, a servant's room.

He believed it was only then, he said, that he came to understand something. Understanding isn't a matter of shifting ideas around in your head, or having feelings. "After all, you always have feelings. You think you're on the side of the poor, that you love them, that you love poverty — as if vague feelings were the same as actions . . . . " It was only then, he believed, that he had come to experience humiliation in his flesh and blood. Up until that time he had only thought he understood.

There was illusion and even pride in being able to choose to live as a poor man among the wretched. Now he was stripped bare without having wished it. To believe you can change your ideas without a change of heart, and that you can achieve this change of heart without changing your life-style, is the illusion of many, an incurable illusion. They continue to be like traveling salesmen, he said, who keep working on their technique: how does one sell refrigerators to Eskimos?

This is how Tonzi gave up wearing his cassock — rather late in the game, after all. He could have done it earlier with official approval, like his priest-friends who were working in factories. For forty years he had worn the cassock: it's not pleasant to have your skin torn off. It clung to him, like all habits. He no longer thought of it as a religious uniform; clerical garb as such had no importance for him. On the other hand, Tonzi didn't have much in common with the sophisticated new breed who believed in the power that came from wearing a tie, just like the others who believed in the Roman collar, and who forgot that the first thing to do is to clear up one's thinking.

One evening the question was being argued in a group, and Tonzi listened to a young liberal priest :

"To be able to say that's a soldier, that's a cop, that's someone who works in a funeral home — all that is useful from an administrative point of view. But a disciple ought to be recognized in another way — by his presence. Real poverty means not having an army or a fraternal union behind you, or a bank deposit to fall back on. Take a close look at the expressions on people's faces.

They don't look at you the same way when you're wearing the uniform as when you're not; even their voices aren't the same. The pious think they know who you are, what you think, what you should say. They make you their accomplice; they ensnare you with their adulation. As for the cynical, they simply don't see you. Because of their mind-set and their prejudices, all they see is the institution. It's crazy, you're just a symbol to them — someone who represents religion, the institution, clericalism, I don't know what — just a functionary of the word. You no longer have a human face; all you have to do is keep still."

"Come off it," Strozzi had thought. "This young Turk is exaggerating. All you have to do to make them forget the uniform is to be stronger than the uniform." Neither ideas nor feelings ever convinced Strozzi, only facts.

Then one evening there was a telephone call. Claude D. had just gotten out of prison. He wants to celebrate the occasion with a few other ex-convicts; Tonzi knows several of them. Claude would like to have a few words with "the Reverend," as he used to call Strozzi. He wants to go straight; in fact, it is to be a farewell dinner. The party takes place in a furnished house on boulevard Ornano. Tonzi finds himself going in at the same time as two streetwalkers. He hears someone behind him saying, "That priest has to have two of them."

The next day Strozzi discarded his cassock and put on civilian clothes. "Oh, he wants to have his fun," the sophisticates said. But there's no point getting mad at them; they're probably going to have to wait for eternal life in order to find out they were wrong. Maybe that's why there are so many people who don't expect much from eternity.

Was it that night, or another? It must have been that night, boulevard Ornano. In the middle of the celebration a man comes in, insists on talking to one of the guests, and demands some money that he says belongs to a woman he knows. Suddenly a fight breaks out, the intruder takes a hard punch to the head, staggers, and falls down dead. At first the doctor wants to refer the matter to the law, then he begins to waver. Tonzi's judgment carries the day — there will be no further investigation. Naturally, there are professions of eternal gratitude, and Tonzi gets the reputation of being beyond the law. The next thing you know, two of the guests, friends of Claude, swept along by his decision, decide to leave the underworld. It wasn't such a great victory for humanity: in five years they found a way to make a fortune legally, but they didn't become any more likable than before — in fact, less so. All they had now were the outward marks of respectability. You're naive, Tonzi; let me say it again.

There was another murder he was mixed up in. It's impossible to be absolutely sure whether Elizabeth's daughter Clarissa was involved. I don't know the whole story; there are lots of gaps in what I heard. In any case, there was a young woman in England, under Strozzi's protection, because her mother wanted to send her away. Yes, he arranged to send quite a few young women to England. Anyhow, while she was at the university the son of a big English industrialist fell in love with Clarissa. It lasted for a year. Vacation time arrived, and he was to come to Paris, presumably to formally ask to marry her. The mother went to a lot of trouble; she wanted everything to have the aura of respectability. Was it at the rue de Levis? Elizabeth bought curtains, knick-knacks.

But the son is a coward. His father insisted he knuckle under, threatened to disinherit him. His son must marry the daughter of a corporation executive. What with the Common Market and international competition, there was no way out. The young man doesn't even have the courage to go

82

alone to see the mother and Clarissa — if it is Clarissa — to tell them. He asks Strozzi to go with him — that's what priests are for, isn't it? The mother gets the news, goes to find her daughter, and tries to explain it to her. One minute the young man is standing in front of the fireplace, the next minute he will be dead. The young woman comes in. She's in a fury, throws herself at him, gives him a hard slap. The wimp topples over an armchair and bangs his head on the corner of the fireplace. Dead on the spot. Rachidian bulb, something like that. What an imbecile!

The family doctor arrives, then the medical expert, and finally the father. A horrible night. The father wants to bring charges; the medical expert wants legal justice. "Give me three minutes, just the two of us," Strozzi says to the father. They go out to the street, they're gone for a quarter of an hour. The father doesn't bring charges.

A few weeks later comes the best part of all: Clarissa wants to be baptized, confirmed, the whole bit; she even wants to become a Carmelite. Strozzi tried like crazy to make her wait. It must have been Clarissa. Elizabeth will still be afraid to talk to me about it at Taussat. An awful melodrama: blood, tears, love, and religion. Hearts that melted.

I could have made up scenes, livened everything up; it would have filled hundreds of pages. My publisher would have been delighted — a sure best seller. Strozzi, we could have made something out of all that craziness.

I'm trying to understand Tonzi's day-to-day life. I'm not going to shadow him but there's a certain contradiction in what I'm doing. I'm forced to listen, to observe, to cross-check, to calculate. It seems he doesn't get more than five hours of sleep.Never gets home before midnight; often it's long after midnight. And the morning? Correspondence. Letters to Marseilles, Dakar, Madrid, Beirut, Hamburg, and London, just as often as to Limoges, Angoulême, Taussat, to villages where some women are making a new start in life. "I love you, Elizabeth." "I'm with you, Eliane." No one is deceived. Tonzi is *le père*, father, brother, friend. Even from a distance, he is bound to them with invisible ties, gives them support.

He's not trying to sell anything. He knows when he can find them at home, away from their turf. He can sit with them in silence for a whole hour, even two. He's simply there, that's all. Or he can carry on a conversation. You could say he pays them regular visits for no other reason than friendship. Someone might tell him that he ought to go see so-and-so; she seems close to a breakdown. Another asks, "Can you find a solution for me? What can I do about my children?"

Education, morality — that wasn't his business. There are others who take care of that. All that interests him is helping someone to live; that's the beginning of morality. His patience is dogged, relentless. He visits one young woman who is neurotic, almost crazy; he comes as often as she wants him. His friends keep telling him he's naive, that she is using him. What does that matter to Tonzi? There's always something to be done, just as there are always excuses for withdrawing. "People who try to deceive you," he says, "they're the ones who are deceived." Tonzi is willing to be the fall guy. One of his "parishioners" has a vision of him as a statue in the church on the rue de Rueil. He lets her rave; she has no one else to talk to. Without him, maybe she'd go crazy. Life doesn't decide to refuse itself, any more than God refuses the breath of life. A saying of Francis de Sales often came to Tonzi's mind: "God has hidden from us the secret of things to come. If we were only supposed to serve those who are going to persevere, the truth is we still wouldn't know how to pick them out from the others. Even if it is only for an hour, we must relieve the pain and sorrow of our neighbor."

As for Tonzi, he always gives the impression that he has done nothing, that he has failed. And sometimes he thinks he's had enough of the Metro, of climbing stairways. He dreams of a house with garden paths and lots of trees. Actually he has friends everywhere who would have welcomed him to their homes as if he were an angel. But he'll never go. Too many unhappy faces float before his eyes. He'll keep taking care of them right to the end. From time to time he spends a day among normal people in Paris; they invite him to their homes, they'd like to protect him. But who is normal?

And what do you think he reads on Sunday? Not *Le Monde*, but the communist paper and a woman's magazine — he even glances quickly at two of the tabloids. Not the serious papers. In other words, he reads what his parishioners read; keeping up with them makes conversation easier, offers some starting points. As for his personal taste, he liked to read philosophy . . . .

The fact that Strozzi can pay visits, have conversations, and help out ten hours a day, six days a week — well, why not? A lot of people are stuck with less interesting jobs. To work with human beings, to intervene in lives, to hold someone's head above water, someone with will power can thrive on such an existence. But those people who wax eloquent on the subject of destitution! Blessings on you, unfortunate ones, for preventing me from seeing myself.

No, all that isn't what amazes me. It's rather, how does one continue to give without developing calluses on your hands — and on your heart? How avoid becoming an entrepreneur, playing the part of a "good" person, turning into a professional of charity? It's the nobility of Tonzi that astounds me. He gives without knowing that he's giving. Never looking down on people, he speaks to everyone as equal to equal, totally oblivious of pity. There's something I can't quite grasp.

I had imagined that, by telling Strozzi's story, I would be feeding a passion I have for underworld vocabulary, the sordid language of gangster stories. Another mistake. Tonzi is absolutely uninterested in all that. I suspect that, even in a physical sense, he doesn't hear it. As far as he's concerned, not just smut but even the trivial everyday language that people use when talking about love, all the accepted words, constitute a language of unknowing hatred, an unconscious revolt against what is a purely interior reality. A revenge against a kind of bondage, it expresses a secret regret at spiritual emptiness, a longing for a friendship that could light up one's existence.

I was going to create local color, rewrite *A Desert Named Pigalle*. I'd put a bold priest in the middle of it all, like in an edifying novel. He'd be efficient, a "fisher of men" — and women, a relaxed type, who'd call everyone Toto. He'd swagger a lot, but otherwise he'd be conventionally generous, genial, with special devotion to the Blessed Virgin, and would hopelessly confuse morality with the moral law, Christianity with First Communion ceremonies. In other words, he'd be an alibi. But Strozzi is another breed.

He does make mistakes. For example, he'll say, "I had to go into the *world*," when he really means *underworld*, It's the upper middle class, or their favorite writers, who use the term "underworld." In Strozzi's vocabulary, *good society* becomes *underworld*, and the *underworld* becomes *good society*. You finally lose track. Must be deliberate on Strozzi's part. Because the underworld is an alibi for respectable society, a kingdom defined by a disease from which they think they are immune, and which they camouflage with worldly rituals. "And I'm an alibi, too," Tonzi insists." Some people who've heard about me like to tell each other, 'Well, there's someone in our circle who's working there, doing something worthwhile.' I'd so much like not to be an alibi."

Jerome Strozzi has no general ideas about the underworld and prostitution. In fact, he doesn't have much confidence in general ideas, any more than he believes in statistics. The underworld? "It's made up of people who are struggling to live, that's all there is to it. One woman may have gotten into prostitution simply because of destitution. For another, it may be a matter of glands."

Strozzi believes human beings have less psychological freedom than is generally believed, but that spiritually they are infinitely more free. I suspect he belongs to the race of "active pessimists," believers who know that the spiritual life can burst forth anywhere, and that there is little difference between vices and virtues. They have completely absorbed the saying of John of the Cross: "It is not the extent of vices or virtues that account for the misery or grandeur of a person; it is the depth of our detachment in regard to our virtues and vices that shows an individual's nobility . . . . ."

"Some women," Strozzi says, "become part of the underworld as a revolt against their family, others have gone through the experience of having been abandoned. And of course there are those who are drawn to the life by a desire for money or luxury. But the worst are those who never go through with their decision. For example, the ones who use a car as part of the scam. The woman suggests a place. The individual jumps in and gets warm. 'I know a place where we can park,' she says; 'we won't be disturbed.' Thirty seconds after they've stopped, a man appears, and suddenly opens the car door. 'Fifty grand or there'll be a scandal.' The passion for money, whether earned legally or not, is infinitely more serious than the weakness of the flesh. But society doesn't want to know about that."

"They're women like all the others, that's what they are. They have a fear of poverty, the desire for comfort, the need for security. A love of pretty clothes. I tell you, they're coquettes like the others. 'Don't you see that I'm wearing a new dress?' they'll ask. They get annoyed at me. 'You're naive, Tonzi.' They say that all the time. I throw it back at them. 'You're the one who's naive to believe all that rubbish.' Then they say, 'You're not a man like the others' — they repeat that all the time.

"And their love of heroes — boxers, runners, cyclists, movie stars — even the Pope, whether they're believers or not. They build a soap opera world for themselves. Like everyone else." It was through these women, he says, that he came to understand the mythologies of the bourgeois world.

"And if one of them leaves the profession, it's a difficult road she sets out on. If she marries, the husband will need infinite patience, a kind of sanctity, for they no longer know what tenderness and caring are. Women who have lived this kind of a life become completely indifferent. Just as it would take a miracle for a writer to produce an authentic work once he has prostituted himself looking for an easy success, it's just as difficult for tenderness to be born in the heart of a whore. You've read Balzac; I don't need to explain all that again.

"And if one of them gets a regular job somewhere, it's a daily battle to keep it. Men get suspicious and pursue their fragile prey. It never ends. They have to leave the offices or factories where they're working, sometimes even their own homes."

A stroke of luck — I met Catherine. She had left the profession, was working in different homes as assistant housekeeper — that is, a maid. Words don't change the reality. Had worked in three successive homes in less than a year. At the end of three months she would have to leave, find some excuse — the husband would keep after her.

I met her later at the home of friends of mine, where she had managed to stay for a year and a half without incident. But some of the guests would look her over, and send her notes. If she went out, the chase began again. So she would stay in the kitchen, hemmed in, bored to death. Letters from Tonzi were no longer enough to keep her going. Finally she declared, "I can't go on living like this; I might as well do things openly. I'll go back to . . . I'm going to see Strozzi. He's like God: he doesn't ask you to give an accounting every day. He lets you live, helps you keep going; he waits."

Among lesbian couples, tragedy is frequently not far away. Strozzi encouraged Eliane to go on living. She was Jewish, an intellectual, read Dostoevsky in the original. She was haunted by the idea of suicide. He held her at arm's length. To get out of an impossible situation, and start all over, she went off to Saigon, where most of her friends were military officers. The chaplain, passing through Paris, had said to Strozzi, "This young woman is a saint; I've never seen anyone like her. Not a single incident, no trouble with men."

"Did you tell him?" Eliane wanted to know.

"No," Tonzi had answered. "A certain kind of saint, that's right. You're a kind of saint."

Elaine began to cry.

Things turned out badly. Tonzi's telephone — how many times had it summoned him! A voice he didn't recognize was telling him to go to a certain address. He found himself in a luxurious apartment, rue de Longchamp. The door was open, no one was around. Then he saw Elaine, lying on the carpet behind a sofa, with a fingernail torn out, a broken wrist, her face swollen, and blood making a black sun on the bright carpet. That night Strozzi decided to write the Dean of the School of Medicine the next morning.

I knew Eliane, I should be able to talk about it. I called her Sonia. I saw her when they wheeled her into the operating room for the second time, saw her smile faintly. I thought of Isaiah: *They have broken and counted all my bones.* Some people from good families had lured her into a trap. They thought, like so many others, that morality is best taught with a stick. They had pushed their logic to the limit. A saint — the chaplain from Saignon was right. With only one true friend, Strozzi. Me, all I'd known how to do was to listen to her talk about Dostoevsky; I was interested in psychology. She was one of the people who pass by very close to you, and because you are too close to yourself, you think you can't do anything for her.

"The prostitute is the tangible sign of the prostitution of the world." That's what Strozzi says. "She lives out openly what many men and women are, in every class of society. Every time a woman or a man, whether in marriage or outside marriage, treat each other as an object, when the bond of friendship is no longer primary, but desire, money, habit, or convenience, there is prostitution. Marriage without asceticism is only a comfortable form of approved prostitution, blessed by society."

I think Strozzi has a special faculty for discerning the same reality under different appearances. His extreme sensitivity to the meaning of people's expressions is almost frightening. I think he senses when souls are dead, but instead of keeping his distance, he comes closer and closer, begins hammering away. A spark can rekindle life.

"Elizabeth, I want to see your eyes light up."

Even when he meets couples, lovers or spouses, who seem affable and have good manners, he's often able to detect signs of domination, subservience, or complicity. He can't help but notice, even in supposedly Christian homes, murderous glances, or a certain tone of voice, sometimes accompanied by kind words. It's embarrassing, for such glances and that tone may be destroying the other person, and Strozzi feels them like a burn.

But sometimes he encounters a profound friendship in which two people are no longer so much man and woman as human beings, equals, persons. Then he feels invigorated, as though by sunlight and fresh air.

He finds flagrant prostitution in journalism, politics, among writers, among those who increase their wealth while defending values — elegant, high class, moral prostitution — just as much as among pornographers and others who exploit vice. Living in the midst of all that, learning to read its language every day as an open book, takes away any desire to judge or classify or label, to ask anyone for identification papers or family pedigree. His mission isn't to find out if people are in good standing with the law. There are others who can take care of that. His mission is to help life be more true. Still, I hope Strozzi isn't being taken in. Many women whom he helped bring back to the world of morality end up like Pâquerette and Sabine, becoming more harshly conformist than society women.

If streetwalkers precede us into the Kingdom, it's not because the Son of man is giving them a reward, but is verifying a fact. The prostitute is more truthful, more authentic, than most of us because of the knowledge and consciousness she has of her wretched situation; because she's more capable of humility. On the other hand, there's no end to the prostitution of the highly placed; they go on pretending, issuing statements, organizing justice, charity, morality, even the love of God, for their own profit. It's all done so skillfully that it takes a miracle, the greatest of all miracles, for a righteous person to awaken to a realization of his wrongdoing and iniquity.

I can still see Tonzi, elderly but ageless, with his unusual, mysterious eyes, one tender and knowing, the other flashing with purple fire. He himself remains serene, as if his case had already been decided, as if he spoke in the name of a sovereign power, as if his anger had become quite impersonal, an aspect of his joy. From the beginning it had seemed to me that was probably the reason there were so few anecdotes about him, no pious folklore. He established no charitable works; he wasn't a philanthropist. Strozzi was someone who reveals, that's what he was. To the famous and the respectable, to specialists who exploit instinct and to experts on moral order, as well as to Christian societies in general, he disclosed their secret vice — practiced in almost invincible ignorance — which consists in treating people as objects. Perhaps that's how we can understand what his clients would say about him: "He's always surprised; he always thanks you." Doubtless that was why he would say, "In just a few years in Pigalle I learned more than in all the rest of my life."

It's all very well to be enthusiastic and praise Strozzi, but I still have to maintain my ironic attitude, and keep my eyes open. I'm skeptical even when the song of praise seems to rise up spontaneously. Is that why Strozzi sometimes says to me, "Your look is like a screen"?

I think again about Pâquerette on Tonzi's lap . . . . Frankly, his serenity gets on my nerves. To explain it all as a mechanism, to unmask an illusion — what a relief that would be! Sometimes I even feel I'm on the side of the nuncio's assistant: "All those women!" Where does Strozzi find the source of his peace? What if that serenity of his were merely satisfaction? If he had conquered temptation simply by giving in to it?

Suddenly, during a digression in the middle of a bland conversation, my throat tightens, star dust explodes under my skin — the truth is about to emerge from yellowish green depths. "It has happened," he says; "two human beings bonded in friendship give themselves to each other — once, only once. They are so carried away that, in complete agreement, they decide upon the impossible: they will separate and offer to everyone whom life sends their way this power of welcome and generosity beyond the flesh.

Who is he talking about? I'll never know. No need to know. It's all too noble: skeptics would find it ridiculous; respectable people would be scandalized. Well, let them laugh, let them complain: there are more truths in heaven and on earth than they'll ever understand . . . . Deep down, however, I don't believe in it. At the same time, it would be worth knowing what I'm really after: the fleeting truth of facts or the reality of a new birth that takes place in the midst of events, a joy that is more like a wound. Am I in a position to weigh what is possible and what is impossible? But we are burdened too quickly in life with words, fears, reflexes, a thousand strange truths. We think we understand human nature and proceed on our way, bent under the weight of our sad wisdom.

Strozzi irritates me. And my reluctance to believe irritates me, too. I feel like that famous writer who, it was said, loved to meet priests and was constantly scandalized by them. They'd hardly have begun to talk than he would eagerly ask the question which, as far as he was concerned, determined everything: "But ultimately, isn't it chastity that . . . . ?"

It was enough for me, however, to see the expression on Strozzi's face for the questions to disappear. Or better, it was enough for me to see him in my memory: his face, his gestures. Words come back to me. Like what he had said to Elizabeth, which had struck her because it was a phrase that Alexander had used: *Don't touch me.* Or the line in one of his letters to her: *Erase me from your thoughts for some time.*

"Lust, yes, he had felt it," he said. He spoke of it as if from a great distance or of a long-ago past.

"Old age is a wonderful time, Sulivan, when you don't take pleasure in the idea of your own death, which separates you from yourself. You don't have to fear it. Age has revealed the greatest joys of my life."

So, before reaching an untroubled love, he had known what lust was. What kind of man would he be if he'd never known it at all? The desire for unity is the greatest force that can lift the world, if its progress is not blocked. The thrust of nature is also the call of God. In a blinding flash Strozzi had grasped the limits of the body, as if the movement of the spirit had to precede the movement of nature.

Gestures, words, and glances try to retain the moment, pure and unsullied. An embrace is a promise of eternity.

How strange that one who drinks of the act nevertheless slips away!

Love, which brings bodies together, isolates consciences.

Men in the underworld tend to speak frankly: they admitted to Strozzi that their relations with women can largely be explained by hate and vengeance. Afterwards, they have a need to sleep — they felt as if they were entering infinity . . . . An intuition of some ultimate boundary — that's what Strozzi experienced: the same need that drove so many men to treat women as their prey kept him at a distance.

An acceptance of limits — not that he was unaware of the grandeur of human love. The union of bodies is an acknowledgment of the lowliness of clay, and the sacrament of friendship extends this union into infinity. It wasn't the road he had chosen, however. In order to give assistance to life, it was necessary to keep yourself, to some degree, outside of life. It was the love of life that kept him from entering its stream. Out of love for life he had chosen the appearance of death. Was he sad that he would have no children?

"No. The children of others are my posterity, a humanity in the making. I have never found the woman by whom I would want to have a child except for this woman that I love, for I love you, eternity, my beloved!"

I hear him laugh. He doesn't go in for lofty sentiments. He repeats to me almost word for word what he had told me the day I questioned him about Paquerette:

"Too much of a sense of metaphysics. Too much metaphysics has probable made me impotent. All things considered, it's even simpler than that: fear, fear of losing the object of love."

My soul is a pendulum. There are times when I listen to Jerome Strozzi as if I'm listening to a master. I no longer argue, I feel like saying "Father." I forget my situation and my past. To pretend to understand pimply adolescents, obsessed adults, and anguished writers suddenly seems a kind of sickness. The real struggle is elsewhere, beyond sex, though often revealed in terms of sex. Of course, a preoccupation with sex causes alienation, but a constant anxiety about purity can easily do the same. Beneath the struggle for purity a more decisive struggle takes place. It is not purity for which we must fight directly, but spiritual liberty.

Nevertheless, my curiosity is always wide awake. I have no frame of reference to understand Strozzi; I've never met anyone like him. Are there perhaps hints in the lives of saints? But, after all, he smokes a pipe. I don't think of him as being especially pious. Or is it possible that his is a new kind of piety? No frame of reference. Can something new be taking place that people wouldn't recognize? For example, a sanctity that resembles nothing already known?

If I ask him if he loves "in the name of Christ", he says that he blames himself for thinking about Christ too much. "In that case, what does the other person become? 'I love you because of Christ?' No. Simply, 'I love you,' nothing else."

Haven't I read the Gospel, he asks? "Didn't Jesus keep saying over and over, 'I must go away'? And at the same time he would proclaim, 'I shall be with you until the consummation of the world.' It is this contradiction which we have to resolve in our inner lives. Christ himself is still an image which separates me, prevents me from loving the other person for himself alone. I don't want to be loved because of Christ, or even because of God. What I want is simply to be loved."

I'm caught. I thought I was the only one who interpreted the Gospel that way. But he lives what I just talk about.

But still, what about his women friends? In what way does he love them? With what kind of love? He doesn't know. What's more, it doesn't worry him, it scarcely interests him.

Doesn't he care about love, friendship, loving friendship, pity, charity? Certainly not charity. He has lost the faith — that is, faith in words like that. "'Charity' has such a sanctimonious air today. It's a word that has become unpleasant for many ears. It doesn't matter that for me it's the most beautiful word on earth. If others understand it as lying, covering up truth, I'm striking it out of my vocabulary. Let no one have the 'charity' to love me!"

It seems to me that, somewhat ironically, Strozzi is watching me from a distance as I struggle with the question of vocabulary. One of the most obvious signs of the spiritual sterility of the West is that in the minds of most people love has only one meaning. Whether in marriage, love, or social relationships, it seems nothing can be acknowledged except this pale, almost abstract, high-flown kind of love in which believers seem to specialize. Everything takes place as if society had conditioned individuals and terrorized them to such an extent that friendship between a man and a woman has become questionable, suspect, and finally impossible.

The true moral law is life. Society has turned morality into something completely external. Of course, conventional morality was necessary for coexistence. Hypocrisy made external relations easier, but such legalism was no help in developing consciences that are alert. Ultimately, the person is the only moral law. Since that has been forgotten, pharisaism has continued to be all-powerful. Some people reluctantly submit to law while others rebel, but everything seems to take place on the surface, not in the depths of existence.

Chastity was considered the great human virtue, but at the same time it was thought that only specialists were capable of living it. They were admired and held in contempt at the same time. Chastity in its highest and deepest truth is everyone's concern: it is the virtue which, according to one's state in life, moderates sense pleasures and guides the art of human relations. An art made up of intuition, freedom, and proportion. But we have allowed ourselves to be terrorized by laws. Following the line of least resistance, we've given in to false social cautions, prudence, often far removed from any interior prudence. We have preferred the lie, or the sadness of artificial relationships fostered by the inhuman moral law of societies, to the difficult, subtle, and inspired art of genuine human relationships, as supple as life. Even very young people are asked to kneel down like camels; then we piled heavy burdens on them and tell them, "Be free, be joyful." They spend the rest of their lives shaking off the yoke, revenging themselves for their false virtue. We talk about impotence. We all think we know what it means. But what about the kind of impotence to which an obsession with genital sex bears witness? Who stops to reflect on the implications of a desire that is more like fear? One thing ought to awaken us to reality: a formal respect for the law in matters of the flesh, just as much as indulgence in orgies, can accompany the most ferocious egoism. Man venerates woman as an idol or flees from her as a devil. But when society, religion or love place her at men's mercy, she is, despite refined appearances, treated as a slave.

When Strozzi writes "Je t'aime" to his women friends he is correcting the established vocabulary, making a frontal attack on an obsession, teaching us how to think correctly. He treats the most tyrannized and downtrodden women as human beings. He demonstrates — no, he doesn't demonstrate anything; he simply proceeds directly to his own truth, already living prophetically in the world to come. So many of the women Strozzi deals with encounter nothing but oppression, noise, and scorn; they should remind us of the condition of millions of other women. Their solitude is unbelievable; they live in a wilderness without friends. Strozzi gives what he can — friendship; he goes to help them, if only for an hour, hoping to remedy the evil.

"A man cannot live without a woman," Strozzi said. "Through her he is linked to the earth. That doesn't mean that bodily relations are necessary, though they represent the normal way offered to the vast majority. Absolute chastity, when it is a free offering, joyous, neither embittered, hardened, vengeful, nor transformed into a driving force for power, is one of life's miracles, the affirmation of a victory of the spirit over the puppet in us. From the outset, by means of friendship, it produces *that* which bonding in the flesh ought to lead to.

"But what about the equilibrium of love and happiness, the psychologists ask, who think they understand human nature but seem to be aware only of the distortions produced by repression. Have they never considered how this contented love they're always talking about could easily be the worst kind of counterfeit happiness, based on the whims of the flesh and transitory feelings? Happiness is not to be found in happiness; it's a consequence. It depends on the object of happiness — if we can use the term 'object' when we are talking about *that* which is present when two beings are one, *that* which escapes unhappiness and death.

"Is chastity impossible? Well, why not?" Strozzi said. "The impossible is the law of life. Whatever there is of greatness in men and women, what is best in a person, is the impossible. God is impossible — but He alone imparts meaning to everything. If pleasure does not lead to the same thing as asceticism, pleasure is only a waste of energy, debasement. If the joy of thinking does not lead us to go beyond thought, thinking is a failure. And if asceticism is only refusal, complacency and pride, asceticism too is a failure."

The gentleness and tenderness that others give each other without always realizing its ultimate meaning, or that they consume in sexual encounters — I think Strozzi gives and receives them without realizing it, or without others noticing. But many are enriched by the process. Intellectuals, people who are governed by principles, can only see onanistic games in all this. Everything unfolds in an area beyond their understanding.

I'm forced to spend day after day hanging around Strozzi, listening carefully to his every word, trying to imagine his life. I suffer from uncertainty, not knowing what to say. Fearful of starting out on an uncharted path, I'm uncomfortable and more than a little disturbed. In all I learned from books I don't find anyone to compare him to. It's as if he had fallen from another planet, had come from a far off time, or perhaps from a world still in the process of being born. I'm afraid of causing a scandal or of getting laughed at, but endure it all in the hope that at a certain point everything will click into place.

One of his remarks comes back to me. In order to explain that the art of human relations is never easy and that asceticism is essential, he said, "Think about Francis of Assisi and Claire. Or remember Francis de Sales writing to Jeanne de Chantal: 'Now, for a time, I must keep a certain distance; I shall no longer see you so often.' Think of all that this sentence implies. One can never simply let oneself go. You must possess your soul — and that's not just a technique. It's an art, a grace, a kind of buoyancy or sweetness that has been won."

At that moment something clicked. Images that I hadn't really noticed previously: Strozzi at Thoissey with his knapsack, retracing all the travels of the saint from Geneva — Annemasse, the chateau de Sales, Thonon, Abondance.

Now I understand what it was that had kept me from paying attention. The man from Geneva had seemed to be a saint of the court, affected, even effete, in his close friendships with women of the world. Astute, yes, a pious humanist, but as foreign to the real life of our time as those virgins, saints, and portraits of Christ produced by the Italian Renaissance, which evolved among the colonnades of palaces and in dream landscapes. That art seemed a perfect reflection of an era which saw Christianity as only a religion, a decoration, a spectacle, a pretext for the beauty of art, justifying the splendors of the establishment. I had begun with a preconceived idea. As I read the life of Francis de Sales, and especially as I turned the thousands of pages of his enormous correspondence, knowing very well that after ten or fifty flat, colorless pages — or so they seemed to me — the meaning would emerge, a cry from the heart or just a thought, excruciating in its simplicity, I now saw Jerome Strozzi take his place among those special lovers who had tried to transcend the fleeting character of love.

I know now what had stopped me. Between Francis de Sales growing up in a chateau among society women, and Jerome Strozzi, a sub-proletariat of

Paris' eighteenth arrondissement, friend of prostitutes, it had seemed to me that there was no possible common ground. Francis was able to give the loftiest kind of spiritual direction, quoting John of the Cross and the great Teresa. Strozzi starts by quoting the Sunday tabloid or some women's magazine — but amazingly, the spirituality is the same, its sovereign freedom identical, their common passion to help life succeed. In place of Madame Acarie, where Francis went every day when he was in Paris — as if to his office — or Jeanne de Chantal in her chateau or later at her convent, or Madame Angelique of Port-Royal, or Madame Sainte-Veuve, Strozzi could only offer Pâquerettes, Elizabeths, Elianes. The words and manners are different but the inner dynamism is the same. It isn't happiness that either one was looking for. They carry others along in their wake; they attract, then hold back their followers in order to lead them further on. They just cannot stop, for they are possessed by *that* which, even here on earth, makes them exist together in the new unity of the beyond. Far from using faith as a protective restraint, they insert it into a lived experience. The other is no longer the enemy, an obstacle, no longer loved in his or her contingency like an object of happiness, but loved in *that* which creates an eternal coming-to-be.

Francis de Sales had achieved directly what we dream about, the desire of poets that Rilke described in his marvelous letters to Merline: "Those irresistible appeals of body and soul, my darling, when will we able to control their violence so that we may rise above ourselves toward something else?"

What impresses me most about Francis is his utter freedom, leaving him both gentle and bold. One time, in the middle of an assembly, when he was already a bishop, he noticed a poor little servant girl, Jacqueline Coste, the only one of his servants of lower estate. He smiled and made his way through the crowd to speak to her, not patronizingly but as a good friend. Equally fearless was his encounter with the beautiful widow, Madame de Chantal, who was wearing many brilliant jewels. He asked her if she was considering remarrying. On receiving a negative reply, Francis told her, "In that case, Madame, you should remove the signs of being available."

His letters don't cheat.   They give evidence of asceticism, mystical experiences, and an absence of sentimental illusions, but that doesn't prevent them from being very much alive. They soar, like all love letters:

> *"My soul is not more dear to me than yours . . . . "*
>
> *"I cherish you as my very soul . . . . "*
>
> *"I offer only one prayer for the two of us, without separation or division . . ."*
>
> *"My dearly beloved, my life--the truth is I was about to write 'Sweetheart,' but that is not fitting . . . . "*
>
> *"I love souls that are vigorous, independent, never weak or cringing . . . . "*
>
> *"As soon as my face is turned toward the altar to celebrate Mass, I no longer have distracting thoughts; for some time now, however, you have been on my mind, not to distract me but to attach me more strongly to God . . . . "*

I am even more pleased that the gentleman from Geneva kept a subtle understanding of our fears and hesitations. It brings him close to us. When he visits the convents of the Visitandines, they ask for news of Jeanne de Chantal. He writes to her: "Your letters are too ardent to be shown to your spiritual daughters who are so eager for news about you. Write me a note that I can give them."

It's not at all surprising that the realists of Annecy understood nothing of this and took revenge for their spiritual impotence. One morning there was a sign on the door of the Visitation convent. In large letters people were able to read:

THE HAREM
OF THE GENTLEMAN
FROM GENEVA

I need to get to know Francis de Sales better in order to understand Jerome Strozzi, instead of looking at him as though he were someone from Mars. Then perhaps I can understand the source of that peace which Elizabeth had found. We intellectuals can't proceed unless we can find analogies, make comparisons. Someone who simply goes ahead without offering explanations is in for trouble. Nevertheless, there are countless differences between Strozzi and Francis. Especially this one: no one hangs a sign on the door of Jerome's convent . . . . Because he has neither convent nor church in which to stay. Some thugs beat Strozzi nearly to death, and then leave him bleeding on the sidewalk.

Once more the day arrives when Jerome Strozzi has to leave his attic room. On the street again, that eternal suitcase in his hand. Hard not to be brushed by the wings of fear when you are in your late sixties and at night you sometimes hear the drumbeat of your heart.

"Jerome Strozzi, are you afraid of death?"

"No."

"What are you afraid of?"

"I'm afraid of that which separates me from death. Of the way I might die. Of being in the way. Of being looked upon as an object. But perhaps it's good to have to go through such humiliations."

People think they've touched bottom, but they go on hoping. Strozzi had surprised even himself by cherishing a dream: two small rooms, which someone had told him about, on rue . . . at the far end of a courtyard. Just what he needed. He could picture himself there already. The owner of the rooms had arranged to meet him early in the morning, at a bar on boulevard de Strasbourg. Meticulous, with the air of a retired captain, the potential landlord was a clerk in the law court of the Seine.

The chairs were still on top of the tables; the waiter was sweeping and whistling softly. The court clerk had carried out a thorough investigation — that was obvious. Strozzi felt himself shrink under the glance of this just man.

"You are a priest?"

"Yes."

"Are you attached to any . . . . ?"

"N-n-no," Tonzi says. "But my name is in the diocesan directory, I believe, yes."

"Does the archdiocese pay you a salary?"

"No."

"Social security?"

"No."

You might say that the court clerk has certainly prepared the scene, but his interlocutor doesn't know that yet.

"Monsieur, in the eyes of the law you don't even exist. You are not solvent. I have no recourse: you cannot have the apartment." Strozzi shrinks like a frozen plant, then the blood rushes to his face, and millions of burning points pierce his skin.

"But M.T. will get it," the clerk continues. "I don't know what sort of man you are, monsieur, and I don't want to know. I've never seen you, remember that. But I can tell you one thing: you certainly have a great many friends among the women social workers at the Ministry of Justice. M. T. is looking for a place. I am renting the apartment to her. She pays me, and people are paying her for you to have the apartment. I have nothing to do with it. First time I've seen anything quite like this . . . . "

Tonzi wanted to embrace the little clerk, give him a bear hug. But it would have been impossible to explain things to him. Anyhow, what good would it do? There are so many things honest men can't understand.

He walked along aimlessly, oblivious to the flow of early morning traffic and its joyous sounds. A positive sign had been given him, an assurance and affirmation he felt he had possessed for a long time, but it was a never-ending revelation. "I have nothing. I am nothing. I hardly exist. I'm free." Joy flooded through him. Its light was dazzling.

I think it was after that day that an unyielding serenity seemed always to dwell within him. For a long time great waves of anger had gathered behind that mask of impersonality — the insurrection of life itself against the roadblocks in his way, against calloused institutions, human exploitation, and every form of pharisaism. There had been so many occasions when he had spontaneously clenched his fists.

Now he was startled to notice that his handwriting was changing. The long, tightly compressed letters of his scrawl were becoming airy, shorter, exquisitely shaped, regular. I'm beginning to understand better that Tonzi's contagious gentleness was a hard-earned triumph.

So that's how Jerome Strozzi survives. Friends, friends of friends, Christians, priests, atheists, Jews, former prisoners, hundreds of women whom he'd kept from drowning — they all chip in. The treasurer of this curious ecumenical parish doles out only what is needed to keep Tonzi in an uneasy equilibrium between poverty and total destitution. The only one who didn't contribute was one well-known Catholic writer whom they approached; people said it was because he was hoping to get elected to the Academy. He is supposed to have solemnly declared: "Let him obey and he will be taken care of" — even the church hadn't asked as much. People like that writer think they have an obligation to protect the church's reputation, as if there weren't already enough beadles to ring the bells. They are just defending the interests of their own clientele. One would hope for something else from a writer: to cry out on behalf of people other than the privileged, to beat down walls with a free voice.

The latest word is that this writer hasn't yet succeeded in buckling on the sword of an Academician. His name? I don't know. Strozzi doesn't betray the one who betrays him.

Tonzi doesn't offer any apologies for his life; he is beyond that. The time is coming when this harsh, sterile world will be suitable only for parasites.

"But listen, Tonzi, this is terrible. You are a kept man."

"So? Who isn't?"

Strozzi is someone who goes on bewildering you. Never a look behind. *A shudder and a dangerous stop.* He just gives a slight twitch when they pull up the ladder of the airplane, or at the moment when he has to go through a door, or relinquish some small, everyday pleasure, with just a valise in his hand. One particular event quite shattered me . . . .

This kind of common reaction is foreign to him. It's our laziness or our anxious attachments that upset and confuse us. We imagine causes as if we were the playthings of chance, of the feelings of others or of our own, pretending that they are evolving without us. But what drags down and destroys one person lifts another up. Events are our war horses. It's true that the past weighs on the present with all its burden, and that time speeds up, dragging us down our slopes. But the past is only made up of our exasperations in the form of thoughts, and our thoughts themselves are nourished by the fears and obstacles that we erect against the flash-floods of life; they are just stories we tell ourselves in order to explain the crazy things we did in our past.

When someone would tell me some new anecdote about Strozzi and it would end with a new revelation, I thought I was hearing the word of life, of the Master of life, the extraordinary word that was pronounced on the threshold of ancient time and to which human freedom is suspended: "Exi. Out! Go, leave your home, your people, separate yourself from all this in order to find yourself."

When a person has found himself, when he has understood both his importance and his unimportance, he becomes free, insolent and friendly. He creates, even invents his past, singing in his own voice the full alleluia of a life teeming with both happiness and unhappiness. Of course, someone who is liberated receives some sharp blows, but privileges would make someone like Strozzi shrink in horror.

It is from these waters that Strozzi must drink his serenity and goodness.

When Strozzi speaks of the beyond, I try to figure out what he means. It's not enough to die in order to attain this beyond, We should be wary of talking about eternity. No one knows what eternity is except that it is absolutely other. "Heaven? I don't know what it is," Strozzi would say; "I never think about it. 'Heaven is the soul of the just.' It's a saying of St. Gregory the Great, if that reassures you. Love wants and demands eternity. The person who refuses that dimension places himself outside of it. It's not enough to say, 'I believe, I believe.' Actions are needed, actions which have to be stretched as far as possible, to an encounter with others. It's a matter of looking with attention, as in painting. A look that either makes real contact or stumbles on an obstacle. That's all there is to it."

One morning I managed to snatch Strozzi away from his correspondence and proposed a walk to the Louvre. I wanted to show him a painting by Cranach, "Young Woman." Actually, I think I just wanted to walk in the radiance of his peace. As a matter of fact, we went to the Petit Palais to see an exhibit. I was caught up in the kind of exaltation that great works of art always give me; I let myself go.

Strozzi said, "You know, a museum is also a kind of cemetery. Just a matter of how you look at things. When all is said, there's not much difference between the spasmodic contractions of love and the devotion of those who are true believers in art."

"You see prostitution everywhere, Jerome Strozzi."

Then he told me a story.

When some intense art-worshiper started to confess his faith, Strozzi would recall a long, bony, scrawny hand clutching his right arm. He would suddenly experience panic, and feel the need to get away.

Years ago, in a public garden one morning, he had met a priest who had just finished saying Mass. It must have been around Easter-time; spring was bursting forth. This priest, who came from a large family, had an immense reputation, almost a kind of glory. He taught at the university, and had published widely. He had a long, dry, clean-shaven face, but there was a flickering hesitation in his glance. A distinguished gentleman, he wore starched cuffs and had gold cuff links. What had there been in the air that day which induced a man like that to give himself away? They had walked for several minutes side by side, keeping in step. The professor was a spry, elderly gentleman. What was it they were talking about? Suddenly the old priest, one of the best known Catholic intellectuals of his generation, stopped short, his long, gnarled fingers shaded the light, and his almost impersonal voice struck Strozzi full in the chest.

"The time is coming, my friend," he said, "when there will be nothing left for us, nothing, nothing but art, art . . . . "

The hand that tightened on Strozzi's right arm was the hand of a drowning man. Strozzi realized that this man, standing in the early morning spring air, was giving voice to his frozen, sterile truth. A desperate longing was digging into him, a void made up of horror and pity. What deep pain had brought him to this point? Strozzi began to imagine he was with Cenabre, the

110

priest-intellectual of Bernanos' *L'imposture*, a living person who was already dead.

I, too, often hear that song, sometimes proud, sometimes humble. Whether it comes from painters, sculptors, or writers, each time it seems that I see the scraggy, fleshless hand of Death. They were people whom I had come to admire, who seemed to have achieved a certain freedom, and I thought of them as powerful. But suddenly I saw them as dry, sterile human beings, with a solemnity that comes with being pontiffs of culture, false priests of a false religion, while they withdrew to an immeasurable distance, exuding a sense of utter futility.

There was little to distinguish them from those wealthy, effete dabblers in art who fill up their inner emptiness, the enormous boredom of their loveless lives, by collecting antiquities as a bulwark against a world that has gone adrift. They are like those women who, no longer capable of seducing us with the youthful freshness of their appearance, cover themselves with glittering, icy-bright objects. It seemed to me that artists like that were betraying life, that they were dead even before they died. What a destiny, I thought to myself: to have painted, sculpted, or written admirable works, works that sparkled with life, from which many have drunk refreshment, and to see them now as empty, nothing but cracked cisterns . . . . But to hear Strozzi expressing my own feelings made them even stronger.

Sometimes I would tell myself that the hands which paint, sculpt, or write are wiser than their brains: the works proclaim what their creators reject. But how can we not feel anguish in the face of their despair, whether it be secret or acknowledged? They look at themselves in the mirror; they are the bards of life, which is inevitably provisional, and have been carried away like a waterfall which clings to the rocky crags. With their hands and voices they hang on like drowning men.

The evening high Masses that are held in the court of the Louvre when one of the celebrities of the art world has died taught me more about this than any confidential observations, and began to take on remarkable significance. What I encountered each time was a declaration, both sincere and feigned, of astonishment, stupor, and the injustice of fate. The Republican Guards, the soldiers, the line of social notables with their masks of grief, mark out a vast square with the coffin placed at the center. Two ushers with silver chains around their necks, looking sad and serious, like the deacon and subdeacon before the Blessed Sacrament, approach the coffin with a gesture of offering, holding a bowl in their hands, an urn, water from the Ganges, a handful of dust from the Acropolis, or whatever. What real presence was it intended to symbolize? There is a flourish of trumpets and a space is opened. Silence deepens as, his step firm and decided, like a boxer walking toward the ring, he comes forward on the moist and shiny bricks, slightly bent over, his head drawn into his shoulders. No, it isn't an aging Gisors who has become a vaguely skeptical collector, or maybe it is a Gisors who now collects on a nation-wide scale, assembles stones, builds the temples of his own faith, inaugurates, preaches, recruits — an apostle, a fighter, who advances to the ambo of this curious liturgy . . . . With arms outstretched, head jutted forward, his hands grasp the wood of the pulpit even before his voice rises and soars, becomes almost inhuman, the voice of a high priest from another age who prophesies, moans, and recites invocations in long, rhythmic incantations. No one feels like laughing. The blood pounds in your throat; prayer springs from your heart at the sight of this man standing there alone, frantically raising his hands to heaven, clinging to nothingness, each time fighting a very personal battle with fate. Nevertheless, it seems he also speaks for all those today who have their backs against a wall of shadows.

I talked and talked, I listened to Strozzi. Our words crossed, were anticipated; sometimes they were enthusiastic, sometimes unjust. We could go on indefinitely, because no one was listening. Those devotees of art, we told each other, attach themselves to images--just like make-believe Christians who create a god in proportion to their panic. Idolaters!

The verse of a psalm came to Strozzi's lips: "The fool hath said in his heart: there is no God." So many artists, writers, intellectuals, builders of new theories, who were venerated in Parisian folklore for debunking the lunacy of mythologies and the childishness of believers, seemed vain and frivolous. For many, art was the last recourse, the ultimate barrier against the absurd. It had become scandalous to see art as anything else. Of course, they still tipped their hats to the faith of earlier ages — "The people who lived then, they were lucky" — but they didn't believe a word of it. They secretly pitied those who were followers of crude fables and lies. They hoped to confuse, beyond recovery, the reality of faith with the natural exercise of human intelligence — which, quite apart from any revelation, requires God just as the eye requires light. Not for a minute did it occur to them that they were building a hypothesis into a certitude. What was missing, ultimately, was life, the demands of life, the very demands that brought a pagan like Henry Miller to the verge of mysticism.

"An old dog never plays," Elie Faure had noted, describing the elderly Renoir who, with rigid, calloused hands, unable to stand up or sit down, a brush tied to his motionless hand, spent the whole day painting vividly colored flowers, fruits, women's warm flesh, the very intoxication of life. Even as a hypothesis the idea had not come to Faure, nor apparently to others, that art could be anything other than distaste for death. Whereas, in fact, it is a secret movement that cannot be controlled, a sign of life hurled beyond itself, capable of awakening a joy that is pure, inexplicable, even in the midst of decomposition. Because people could not see this, art has become culture, and so many artists and writers have simply produced objects for consumers. Art used to have nothing to do with culture. Creators used to create; they didn't worry about enriching the patrimony of humanity. Artists no more thought about culture when they were creating than true Christians thought about religion when they dedicated themselves to God. What they wanted — at least artists worthy of the name — was to exist, to crack open the doors of the impossible, to communicate with other minds that were emerging into glorious life. Do a man and a woman who give themselves to each other have the pious intention of increasing the human race? No, they're looking for happiness, even if their happiness takes the form of a particular face.

I'm unfair, Jerome, but let me be unfair. True works of art reveal a refusal of death. They are a powerful attempt to crystallize life against time — which, of course, is irretrievable, but that is only a superficial viewpoint. More powerful than ideas, more powerful than convictions which can be a barrier, great works of art tell us that, just as the crest of the waves becomes golden in the evening sunlight, life, too, is prophetically luminous.

It was not a question of ideas and arguments, but of experiences as real as emptiness and nothingness . . . . A person who truly creates can test this: intuition, awareness of a beyond which is intrinsic even to one's actions, the bursting forth of an instant to reveal a kingdom. Just as someone in love can discover not just a provisional salvation but eternity in fidelity, so death can become something other than catastrophe. It can be a dazzling radiance. In this perspective, works of art become sign and promise. Time can gnaw at them, but it's of no importance since they will have accomplished their mission. No need to chase after them, or set up a refuge for them. There will always be enough works of art to call forth new makers, new creators, in each generation. The rage to collect, to file, to explain, to know, the mystique of culture, reaches a point when it becomes an obvious symptom of sterility. Strozzi had been right to call it prostitution. Everything was happening as if life had become afraid and stopped to contemplate itself. Art became a spectacle and a diversion, just as religion had. That's hardly surprising when people no longer believe life can transcend itself. Nevertheless, life goes on saying *exi*, go out, leave, extend yourself; don't get fixated on love, or art, or death or religion. Go to the very limits of yourself. Have confidence in your dreams.

"You know, Strozzi, you ought to watch TV from time to time. One evening I caught an interesting program. Giacometti had just been decorated, I'm not sure what for. It certainly wasn't one of those solemn ceremonies at the Louvre. There he was on the TV screen, stammering; you could see he wasn't used to all the publicity. It was fantastic. You could sense he really had too many things to say. All at once he began to tell a story . . . . Things took off. 'Suppose,' he began, 'that I had a Rembrandt or a Rubens in my house, a masterpiece, and that a cat was caught behind it. Please realize that I have no great love for cats. But suppose that it's impossible to move the oil painting. What if it were necessary to slash it in order to save the cat? I wouldn't hesitate for a second. I'd believe that I'd be doing a good act. And as I said, I don't like cats.'"

"That's just the point," Strozzi said. "A person must not be afraid to tear down idols. For me, what's especially important are mental idols. Principles, the ideas behind which men and women are dying of thirst. I like your sculptor — what's his name?" A minute later, he added, "You get too worked up. Art must be a terrible temptation for you . . . . For me, art is mostly a memory. I have other things to do."

It had been a happy morning, tossing words and ideas into the Seine. The little yellow leaves of the poplars along the river bank shimmered in the luminous air. The violet buds of the plane trees along the quay were about to explode. *At this sign you will know that summer is nigh.*

Jerome Strozzi has other things to do than get involved with art. At times it seems to me that we are evolving in two worlds that are foreign to each other. Another kind of alienation keeps him fully awake. It's useless to try to find out anything about his various encounters; he's not interested in providing material for stories about himself. He gave me his soul, not that of someone else. So I have to be content with memories of memories . . . . By chance, however, there was an exception. Walking down rue de Torcy, he said, "I've got to stop here for only a second. I'm just going to let someone know I'll be there tomorrow."

Someone who wants to do a study of destitution doesn't need to go to India. Just pass through the very proper facades of Paris streets and enter the courtyards, whether in the eighteenth district or elsewhere. The room is disgraceful, the window doesn't close, the fireplace doesn't draw, there's water on the landing. Arletta is eighty-six, thin as a skeleton, toothless, her face blackened from smoke, wrinkled like a frozen apple. You can find old women like Arletta in India, in the arcades of the temples. Horror is stronger than pity. I cough, my eyes water; in the smoke nothing can be seen. Strozzi is completely at ease. Arletta takes his hands. He embraces her. A shudder goes down my back.

But suddenly I see her eyes — the radiant eyes of a child, lifted toward this man's face. The ugliness is gone. He talks to her as an equal, without the slightest trace of condescension. For Tonzi she is his mother, his daughter, his sister. It's Thursday. He says he can't stay today, but that he will come tomorrow. Choking and crying, I pull him gently by the sleeve. I'm behind Tonzi at the door; it's impossible to rush him.

Arletta holds me back by the arm, singing his glory. "My dear sir, for the last ten years he has been coming to see me every Thursday, and when he can't come, he stops in to tell me or he sends someone. We're old friends. I think he likes to talk with me. Do you know, when he found me, I couldn't even walk any more? Some of my toenails were at least three inches long. He came back with one of his women friends. They heated water, cut my toenails, and rubbed my feet. Look, over there is the basin, all polished and shiny. Do you know Strozzi very well? I wonder what he sees in me. I had begun to believe that no one would ever love me again." That's what she said, almost word for word what Elizabeth had told me.

At this point I began to feel sick; maybe it was the smoke. And yet, as absurd as it seems, one of Beethoven's melodies began to turn around in my head:

> *If you wish to give me your soul,*
> *Let it be in secret.*
> *And as for our love,*
> *Let no one be able to guess it.*

Tonzi had slipped away a long time ago. And I'd been looking for motives, was going to explain everything psychologically. Served me right. But after all, he could have put the little old lady in a rest home. I told him that when

I caught up with him on the sidewalk. He had tried, he said. Nothing to be done. It would have been the death of her.

While we were walking along in silence, it finally came to me: Strozzi was simply in the service of life, any life, no matter how humble or desperate. What was that other declaration of Tonzi which Elizabeth had repeated? "I want to see your face light up" . . . . With Arletta he was simply there. He didn't talk about her soul or about God. He seemed to live with the strength and power of a man who had been brought back to life. All that he was good for was to rekindle light in eyes that had become dead. Meanwhile, he was paying the price.

Now I will recite the "stations" of Strozzi for you. There will be no procession, no discourses or homilies, no commemorative plaque. Boulevard Barbès: wounded. Rue de la Nation: beaten — also on rue Lepic, two steps from the Moulin Rouge. The most spectacular case, rue de Chartres: thrashed and left for dead among the garbage cans. They find him in a bar; next thing he's at the hospital, and the police and the doctors are asking him questions. His friends want him to bring charges but in that district you don't bring charges. A streetwalker asks him for help. So that's what he does, no questions asked. And of course, those who make their living from flesh and blood respond by teaching him a lesson. That's all he has to say about it.

He gets swept up in police raids. Place Clichy. Boulevard Rochechouart. Suddenly there's the police van--pin-pon, pin-pon . . . . Once he was taken into custody at the Prefecture. Another time at the police station on rue

Ballu. There he was, along with North Africans, streetwalkers, and their pimps, those under restraint — in other words, among his friends, people who call on him for help in a crisis. The officers at the rue Ballu station take him for a false priest.

"All right, buddy, what do you do?"

"Priest."

"Oh, excuse me, Father — hey, how can I be sure of that? What proof do you have? You're not wearing the Roman collar."

"Telephone Barbet-de . . . . "

"What's that?"

"The archbishop's office — something like the Prefecture for the church. Look it up in the phone book. It's B-a-r . . . . "

"Well, you look all right."

They telephone, wake up someone.   A voice says, "It's not possible, a priest in a police raid! We'll look up the name . . . .   Oh my, I guess he is . . . . "

"There you are," the cop said. "They don't seem too happy about you, Father. As far as we're concerned, it doesn't make any difference. Everybody has to have a little fun from time to time."

The chief arrives and takes a protective attitude.

"We'll take you home in a car."

"I'm big enough to go by myself," Strozzi says. "Or take all the others home too."

"What are you talking about?" the chief said. "You're a rotten priest."

You've forgotten, Tonzi, that a priest is supposed to be an early-to-bed person, a prominent member of society. Why do you hang around with publicans, sinners, gangsters, and streetwalkers? That's what we have police for, along with medical experts, and at the end, the morgue. I feel like singing a little song for you, a song without rime or reason. Music, please.

Where will they take you the next time
  that you fall on the sidewalk?
Who will ever know that, after all, you were fragile,
  and like everyone else, timid and bewildered?

But people will say: he's imprudent.
  All he had to do was to keep quiet, stay out of trouble.
The pitcher that goes too often to the well
  Will come a cropper at the bottom of the ditch.
The guy didn't steal it,
  That's what we tried to tell people.
My God, all over the world
  people always say the same thing.

When a man begins to stand up straight, please don't say
  "You're imprudent, you're proud."
Say, rather, "Maybe he couldn't do otherwise.
  Perhaps he didn't know how to bury the talent he had received."

You wise men, what is the value of your wisdom
  if you just remain seated among your equals,
commenting on the wisdom of nations,
  doing your best, out of pity, even out of charity,
to render the cross inoffensive?
  —yes, that scandalous cross on which He died
like a slave, like a criminal . . . .

You tender hearts, the truth burns you.
  How well you know how to invent reassuring words—
Sweet-talkers who bury your treasures.
  A little of this, a little of that. A little parsley,
a little salt, a little pepper:
  serve warm. But no scandal—
Let this be just between us.

You inform against those who advance under fire.
  The calumnies rain down, while they stumble and fall.
They are covered with dust and mud.
  For they have set forth on paths that were not yet staked out.
They are wounded and destroyed

because they entered the jungle.
  Scribes, great Masters,
you have stayed on the national highways,
  the roads everyone walks on, on which
the seed of the sower dries up and dies.

You will preserve your life;
  you will grow old, peaceful and revered.
You will receive applause and chairs of honor,
  and the medals the world reserves for those who serve it.
But the Father will descend from the highest hill
  in order to come to the lost children.

The next day, the music is over: Strozzi is summoned to appear at Barbet-de-Jouy, Embassy Row. When you are a priest, it is simply not done, to get swept up in a police raid.

"Why not?" Strozzi asks. "There are sons and daughters of God caught up in those raids every night, while you are sleeping."

The officials at the chancery office hadn't thought about it that way. They had forgotten that the Son of Man had allowed himself to get picked up one evening . . . .

What is amazing is the way Tonzi would call on his mother every time he was in a crisis. Who else could he call on? Who would listen to him? And even though she thought of herself as mother church, she wasn't very cordial either. How is it possible? She lives in elegant quarters, behind walls padded with silence. She has connections, has had centuries and centuries of time to establish them. But what does it matter? Whatever the case, Tonzi himself is full of gratitude since she supports him, has never denied him. That's all he asks of her.

Another image of mercy comes to mind. We need a closeup of Constanzi's hand on Jerome Strozzi's shoulder. He's still living on the rue des Roses at that time. Constanzi had already visited the community. The papal nuncio Valerio Valeri had heard of him, so Constanzi, a counselor at the nuncio's residence, was asked to visit this strange priest who went around dressed as a common workman.

"Oh, it's you," Constanzi says. "The last time I came to have lunch with you I took you for the cook's husband. Anyway, I thought he was O.K., that husband. I said to myself: they're lucky to have found such an employee. *Amico mio*, this time I'm taking you to a restaurant, the Lutèce. It's better for the *conversazione, va bene?*"

Tonzi had never been to a restaurant like the Lutèce. So they have lunch. Strozzi does the talking. I'd give a great deal to know what he said. But I can imagine the round, benevolent face of Constanzi, flabbergasted, incredulous. The paradoxes of the Gospel actually being lived out. Impossible.

When they get up from the table I see Constantzi's left hand placed for just a minute on the right shoulder of the old veteran. What does this almost furtive gesture mean? "My dear, dear friend, where are you going?" While he lifts his right arm and then lets it fall back. Or perhaps: "Don't count too much on us to get you out of a tight spot. Or was it "Courage! After all, we're in this together"?

In Constanzi's eyes I think I read a fleeting, haunting melancholy. It's sad to be just a dignitary in the system.

Strozzi never forgot that hand. Although it didn't promise any particular help, still, it was a maternally caring hand.

On the Mount of Olives, on that night of Jesus' agony, it was necessary for the disciples to sleep. *Dormite jam et requiescite.* Sleep now and take your rest. On the lake, however, during the tempest, the Son of Man goes on sleeping while the others are wide awake with fear. During the agony in the garden, the Son of Man is awake and the disciples sleep. I am at one with the disciples, sluggish and sleepy.

Someone, however, has to cry out. That's my job, to be the town watchman, the one who alerts the public. The disciples must sleep while the sons of men continue to pass by the cross without seeing it. But those who have to cry out, let them cry out, those who are supposed to bless, let them bless; let the doctors of the church dogmatize, let the great masters of thought contribute to the deception with false adulation. Everything has to come together — acceptance and rejection, necessity and the revolt against necessity, prayer and blasphemy. The night of agony must come to an end in the morning.

One day I tackled him head on. "Strozzi, where do you stand? What do you think about God?"

"What do I think, Sulivan? What the Bible and the church tell us. But you have to understand: we're dealing with concepts. All these ideas — they're only a kind of insurance, like a mountain-climbing rope, or a parachute. Most of the time, you don't think about the rope or the parachute; if you did, you wouldn't make it. I haven't yet begun to understand the things they say about God. Besides, there's a danger in understanding too fast, in thinking you know all about it. Of course, it's useful in bringing about a superficial unity among believers. It isn't God who is difficult; it's men and women who are varied and complex. To say that God does not exist is hardly any more inaccurate than to say that He does. After all, whoever states that God exists risks making Him an element in the world, a phenomenon, a handy object. The *Nada* of the Spanish mystics makes more sense to me. Or, if you prefer, the Hindu fulness, fulness in the form of emptiness. God is the impossible, the immensity of the possible, the love beyond life which is at the heart of life, *that* to which life aspires.

"You want to know where I stand in regard to all this? I don't know anything about it. And I'm not interested in knowing. I hope to have the grace — watch out, grace can easily be one of those tag words Molière has fun with: it can mean nothing. For me, however, grace is that which pushes life further onward as soon as you stop being self-important, hanging on to what one is, or what one has. As I've often told you, I instinctively see Jesus, Son of God, in every human being. God has no other image except the face of a person, every person."

"If you had been given an order either to obey or to leave the church, what would you have done?"

"Don't ask me false questions," Strozzi says.

For Strozzi the weight of the church, the limitations of its institutions — all that is normal, predictable. Institutions are simply not his specialty. There are lots of others who can keep them going. Those who get involved in new approaches or fill new ministries have to expect suffering and loneliness — it's like a law of nature.

"People like me are possible only because there are all the others."

"Jerome Strozzi, quote me the first phrase of the Gospel that comes to your mind."

"'I am the life.'"

There's no hesitation — the answer flashes out. In dealing with the men and women he encounters every day, he has the heartbreaking sense of a humanity that is not quite human, but which desperately longs to be so.

When he's about to meet someone, he has just one prayer: "Through me, let her find what she is looking for. Let me try to be the other, and bring to life in myself what, in spite of appearances, is true in her." Strozzi has a love for life even in its lowest manifestations. On its every level he has an intimation of *that* which transcends life's limits. It's not that he's striving for some kind of ecstasy that will overwhelm him. No, Tonzi isn't a writer, nourishing himself with his own light.

"You seem strangely lacking in a sense of moral law."

"A sense of moral law," Strozzi repeats slowly; "I don't know what that is. I suppose I have one; it's possible that I do, unconsciously. When Ian Smith says, 'There are thousands of men in Rhodesia who are prepared to tighten their belts in order to save our values,' he has a sense of the moral law. Well, try to figure out what that's worth. Each one of us, each group, each class, has a special way of acting and of living. For a long time now the people with power wanted us to believe that their moral law was the only true one. They had a monopoly on morality. But what interests me is this: what seems immoral to us is actually moral for a particular individual. After all, the gangster has his moral code, and so does the prostitute. You have to start with that, and to be ready to set out along with them, beginning today, over the long road traveled by history and the Bible.

"You have to accept living persons on their own terms, with their own reality. Instead of flinging values at their head, you have to take them where they are, whether on the level of instinct, or law, or freedom. As for values, I don't know what they are. Yes, I do: they're idols. The moral law doesn't exist in some cut-and-dried form when you are dealing with human beings. 'Order is already present,' Claudel said. 'Why torment yourself when it's so simple to obey and when order is already present?' But order is not a simple given. Laws are not the work of some director-general, administered by delegates. Morality comes into being when life calls out to us. It is created and brought into existence within the agony of history by each individual in turn, not in some arbitrary fashion, but organically.

"'The marvelous kingdom of humanity!' How can those who talk like that make the person simply a servant of the moral law? Do they leave any room for eternal life, which is supposed to have already begun? They turn people into slaves here on earth and then tell them, 'You will be kings in the life to come.' As if all you needed was to die! That's not what Peter, Paul, or John said. They speak of the Son of Man, of the person who asks to be born. He was born, but it's as if he hadn't been. What has been said is true for all times, but it's as if it had never been said. You have to break through the ideology to find life again. You have to forget the principles so that you can grasp and understand them at the very heart of existence, in their original state, warm and glowing.

"Why are you forcing me to explain myself? Everything escapes me when I try to put it into words; it becomes false and ridiculous."

We have to take a stand. Tonzi is not a pillar of society, a defender of values. For myself, I was overwhelmed. I had thought about so many of these things, but only abstractly, not fleshed out, in the typical way of would-be philosophers. And now I was finding these same ideas in a man who had begun by living them, had discovered them without the help of books, at the heart of lived experience.

For example, the idea that religion can make people inhuman. It seems to me that this is what the modern world has come to suspect, sometimes saying it out loud, more often leaving it unexpressed but implied. Reduced to the level of group-think, Christianity transformed itself into a natural religion.

Specialists defined, clarified, and commented on this phenomenon. It was left to ordinary men and women to reconnect with the mystery at the heart of Christianity, whatever they made of it. But to start out by assuming total clarity in order to assent to darkness — that's a strategy which assures that you lose even before beginning. Anyone who speaks in the name of enlightened ideas or a system can only be seen as an oppressor, a colonizer of the spirit. The revolt of the human conscience against such a religion is a sign of health. Real believers should be delighted by this protest.

Don't complain that I'm undermining theology or law. All I'm saying is that we must interiorize them enough to forget them. We must stop using theology and law as instruments of control, unless we want to produce a world of slaves — and ultimately of rebels. Tonzi is right, Reverend Fathers: poverty is not a matter of whether the cross you wear is made of gold or wood, or whether or not you own an amethyst or an American car. Poverty begins in the depths of one's existence, in the language and style which emerge from the depths of night. Poverty springs from the heart, out of an experience that remains unformulated, in words still heavy with darkness yet shining with light, the only kind capable of evoking friendship and a taste for the impossible.

I've been searching a long time for words to describe Strozzi: generous, bold, independent. It's crazy how the mania for analyzing and classifying almost never leaves me. Someone who withdraws from society and breaks with its prejudices — of course he's going to be different. Think of an artist who has maintained — or rediscovered — a childlike perspective, who doesn't see things in the ordinary way. The crowd simply does not understand him. They only know how to see what they have already seen. It's the same story with a person who has a deep interior life. She becomes a puzzle as soon as she plunges into the very depths of the soul, and when she returns to everyday existence again, she seems enigmatic. When we hear about the Curé of Ars lighting his fire with bank notes, we think he's crazy. And Catherine of Siena shows an equal lack of common sense when she spends the night talking to an assassin, and accompanies him to his execution the next morning, receiving his head in her hands. We're amazed at Francis de Sales when he breaks his fast by peacefully munching nuts — which makes it impossible for him to celebrate Mass. From his point of view, it was more important to give pleasure to the friend who had presented him with this gift. And we have just as hard a time understanding the Son of Man as he approaches the fig tree.

You remember that day when Jesus, followed by his disciples, comes upon this fig tree which has no fruit. Jesus curses it, even though the Gospel says "it was not the season for fruits." Voltaire lets out a guffaw. Bertrand Russell, one of the leading thinkers of our time, is exultant: "Look at what Jesus did; he was neither wise nor even very smart." And there's nothing more enlightening than to tell the story of the fig tree, or any of the hundreds of paradoxes in the Gospel, to respectable Christians: their faces are suddenly overwhelmed with incomprehension, bewilderment, even panic. They're like cattle on a cement prairie. As if what Jesus was talking about were figs! In fact, the story challenges all of us who are so quick to plead necessity or common sense, to defend our habits or our laziness, so clever at offering explanations, so ready to justify, to erase, to invoke time or age or the season as excuses. Men and women are made for the unexpected and the impossible — the Gospel keeps reminding us of this. We may even have to pluck out our eye in order to see. "God" means there is nothing that's impossible.

It seems to me that Strozzi never stops thinking about that sterile fig free.

People like Strozzi have so much to teach us. More, in my opinion, than those pale, thin scholars who are always manipulating ideas, adjusting the slogans of the tribe, or the assistant lecturers, or those who compose glossaries. Strozzi has plunged more deeply into life, restored flesh to it; that must be what gives him such a noble bearing, why he's able to spread this inexhaustible happiness all around him.

I compare two photographs that have been rediscovered, that he doesn't know about. One of them, taken just after he came back to Paris, shows him wearing the clerical cassock. His cincture is carelessly loose, and he looks like a plucked crow, dispirited and sad. In the other, twenty-five years later, I see a shining prince, holding a child and laughing. What spark kindled that fire? Here is a representative of a new race, a slave neither of principles nor of a system. A priest, visible and invisible, of the catholic, apostolic, and Roman church, visible and invisible. Yes, that's what he is, neither a functionary nor a solicitor nor a preacher, but a member of the invincible race of those who have risen from the dead. A staretz, a guru, he flows along with an amorphous crowd, with that race of artists and realistic mystics who transform desire into love, fever into illumination, and ideas into bread and wine, who bring the beyond into reality.

I try to understand. If I walk in a museum or along the sea, if I climb a mountain, if I write, not if I pray but if I am caught up in prayer without realizing it, no longer aware of my body with its weight and ugliness, then I am in Jerusalem. I fall back so quickly, however, and forget. But Strozzi, is that what he experiences every time he's helping someone, when he loves? I think of him as he goes through his days — invulnerable, freed from himself, having surrendered without conditions. He has entered into an active, contagious serenity, the great happiness of mid-life, "the joy of a man fully alive, who is the glory of God."

At a time in their lives when most men have built shells of armor or have become frightening beasts of prey, clever at acquiring, winning, convincing and dominating — unless they're beginning to tremble at the thought of judgment falling due — I'm quite impressed if some one straightens up and sets out on his journey, rejuvenated. The true birth of a person takes place when the spirit takes over — not thoughts, not ideas, but spirit — when prejudices fall like dry fruit under the wind of liberty, because mental attachments are more fatal than those of the flesh.

Death does not always come just at the end of a life. There are a great many living dead among us, people who exist only as part of the crowd, content with merely being on stage in the theater of the world. Those who have not awakened, who have become rigid in their values and principles, vices or virtues, who are intent on making themselves believed, have betrayed their baptismal names, even though they pose as venerable defenders of the good, the honored, and the blessed. They have not yet been born.

People are born only at the moment they come to terms with spiritual liberty. But who practices spiritual liberty, who really tests it? The Christian world seems to have patiently accomplished the feat of transforming the most scathing part of its message, Paul's song of liberation, into an object of sickly hymns and mental illusions, a refuge for misfits, leaving atheism to rediscover

131

the explosion of liberty at the heart of life. It may be a wounded liberty, rootless and absurd, but it is still exciting enough to take the place of faith for entire generations, with great leaders, with both prophets and false prophets.

The Christian world had grown afraid. It wanted everything to be in order, smooth and shiny; it wanted to reconcile the taste for power and prestige with interior liberty and freedom. When Christian liberty becomes the heart of people's existence, they lift up their heads and raise their voices. Like animals who panic and turn tail, who can smell danger faster than the wind can carry it to them, the scribes and pharisees showed an obstinate and endless patience as they strove to immunize and neutralize society against the threat of liberty. For joy, which is born of freedom and only from freedom, is a deadly peril. It shakes walls, enlarges the soul, strips off old skins, and tells the stranger, the blacks, the Chinese, "You are my brother, my sister." To the atheist it says, "We share the same unbelief"; to the prostitute, "You are no worse than many others; in fact, you're more honest." With its sense of humor, joy sees Christian liberty as rooted in faith; in its winnowing-basket it sorts out what is alive and what is only of archaeological interest. Leaving the past behind, joy strains toward the future, treating what has been already been achieved as of little value.

As long as liberty and joy could be restricted to rituals, to certain special days and designated times, the defenders of religion were content. Since it would be too risky and too costly to allow freedom to intrude on their everyday life, they decided to live only on the outside and fell back on official ceremonies, reassured by the good will that such observances presume. They hoarded much of their energy by not really living, and used it up by practicing extreme caution while taking close notice of others. It's hardly surprising that so many have left the church without regret or remorse, deeply convinced that they were being faithful to the best that was in them.

A person is alive only to the extent that she achieves spiritual freedom, radiating the spirit of alleluia, no longer responding to external commands, having become one with God — who never gives an order because He is love. Civilization, culture, the Vatican, the pope, and the church exist only in order to permit each of us to become alive and free. I think people like Strozzi do more to expand human space than the cosmonauts. What he represents is the leaven at work in the dough, which will take some time to ferment. People like Strozzi are opening up the spiritual space for a new renaissance.

You think I'm just wandering. Well, what difference does it make if Jerome Strozzi isn't exactly as I've presented him? I haven't sounded his heart, or tested his back. I sing of an unknown, an adventurer of the open spaces. There is a Strozzi sleeping in every one of us, a Strozzi waiting to be born.

One night I had the urge to take a look at the places where Strozzi hung out. Pigalle, Clichy. I wasn't going there looking for intimate revelations or personal secrets; I had enough of those. I wasn't intending to offer pictures of wretched lives complete to the smallest detail. Enough writers have cashed in on the subject of morality and immorality. There's no need to drink all the water in the sea in order to know whether it's salty: one swallow is enough.

So I let myself be carried along by the crowds in the streets. It was pleasant enough, mingling with so many people under the streaming lights. What does it matter if the cities are drab, the streets mean and ugly, so long as we bring them a beauty from deep within us? Inner warmth can make those cold, hard streets friendly.

Try to be receptive, I told myself. There must be a secret meaning in all this noise and tinsel . How can it be connected with human aspirations? I look at everything intently, with every pore of my skin. The city crackles and throbs with its artificiality; I'm no better off because I know it's money that keeps it going. So much the worse for the city, but for the moment I'm happy in it. The streets and the faces of the people seem to speak to me.

I hear the sea — why is it that I can't see a crowd without hearing and seeing the sea? Why can't I see the ocean without imagining crowds? I hear the sea; I'd like to know how to use a camera to catch all the colors and compose an abstract picture. The crowd comes and goes like the sea, like blood that comes and goes into the arteries and the veins, seeking an exit, hurling itself at its limits. Human flesh fills the night streets, a great mass of flesh, divided, quivering with excitement, driven back by the same breakwater, picked up again by the tide of life, of death, every morning, every evening, in each generation. It's as if human beings had no substance of their own, as if movement were the absolute, and living beings, in the image of the non-living and of the sea, were in search of their very being. Each person, tightly closed in on himself, looks as if he forms a separate unit, as if he knows where he is going. But the countless bodies who look as if they know what they want, that flash out and then decline — a Danube, an inexhaustible Mississippi, constantly fed from innumerable springs — are enlivened by movements which do not come from within them. This tender, fragile human flesh continues to be born, to suffer, to enjoy, to die, here, there, and everywhere, among songs that proclaim that it is good to stay close to one another and embrace, that none of this can last, that one must hurry, that one is lost and then found again.

Perhaps that was what Strozzi felt, before making any judgment: astonishment in the face of that which is rather than being for or against anything, the secret hope at the strongest point of the tide.

The swell of ideas and feelings was surging, the ebb and flow, diastole and systole of the crowd in the streets, of the sea, of blood in the arteries, of ideas running through one's head. Things are going badly, that's obvious. It will be cold tomorrow, or hot; there are, there will be, deaths, sicknesses, despair. Our youth has flown away; there's no longer a sense of morality; the situation is desperate but not serious. Everything is moving toward its end but the heart of the world is still beating; a song rises up again as soon as there is a free person somewhere, and the music holds up quite well.

But you would have to pay no attention to individual destinies, you would have to be blind to faces. To what austere delight had Spinoza introduced me, at a time when I thought I had almost succeeded in turning my heart to stone: *Non ridere, non lugere, nonflere neque detestari, sed intellegere.* Not to laugh, not to weep, not to detest, but to understand. In the face of every evil and even death it was only necessary to get a little perspective in order to understand — that is, to adhere to necessity by locating the particular within the universal. For a time this strategy preserved a frozen peace. Sooner or later, however, life brings an incurable wound that leaves you dazed and humble, turning you from Athens to Jerusalem, bringing you to your knees. *De profundis clamavi!*

You would have to pay no attention to individual destinies; you would have to be blind to faces. Hour after hour sad Maenads mechanically go through the same gestures, seeming almost not to exist, existing only because of a glittering triangle of jewels that conceals *nada*, that void of nothingness. Watch those old people, their sharp, frozen faces stretched toward the waves of young flesh as if toward some kind of deliverance; notice the lifeless, dead eyes of the women.

Jerome Strozzi's discerning look was making its way within me. The musty smell of infinitely tired lives ended by falling on me — the phosphorous of aborted desires, the acid-sweetened fermentation of corrupted souls, the sound of bank notes crackling under one's fingers: it's not necessary to starve, you can enjoy a little luxury, plan for an honorable existence in old age, or restore your virginity at all-night strip-tease bars and shabby hotels. Spit, scratch, or starve. How do you cross these streets without a curse or a prayer on your lips? Here the traffic is in blood and sperm.

But the pimp has a soul, too, and his own fears and hopes. Why shouldn't he have the good luck to find a friend who would show him the emptiness of things? Some pimps whom Strozzi knows are no worse than other people who work in legitimate businesses. The pimp would like to have his own shop, his own clientele, a desk, a beautiful, legitimate wife covered with diamonds and swathed in mink; he'd like to show her off like an American car, offer his reflections on world affairs to universal approbation. He'd like to take his greyhounds out in the evening after dinner. But he's in a tight spot; no time now for values.

Here, I said to myself, are the stereotypes of love, the theater that epitomizes so much of our world. Of course, there are other theaters: hospitals, for example, a permanent theater, where at this very moment uremia patients are howling like animals. And in the "theaters of operation," as they are called, soldiers keep the peace, machine guns strapped across their hearts, and others shudder in trenches, as bombardiers of Christian civilization discharge their seeds of war for the salvation of the world. Does all this ascend among the spheres like celestial music?

But here is the theater of love that concentrates under its floodlights, crystallizes, and simplifies, the better to reveal the secret truth of distinguished societies that are well policed, knowing almost to the millimeter what one can and cannot show, say or not say, a truth which has greater impact because it has been isolated. Both rich and poor, pretending it is a foreign, exotic world, come here to contemplate this truth: that everything is bought and sold — pleasure, the illusion of an hour, a night, a lifetime — while white rockets calm the strong desire to run away, to pull down the stage scenery, to surrender, heads still buzzing with innocence, and hearts beating too quickly. The walls collapse and crumble: there is a false delirium, followed by circus cyclones and cries of liberation that attest to an inexorable servitude.

Individuals change but not the crowd, brushing against one another, dancing the fox trot or coiled in a slower movement, star dust on their soft shoulders, eyelids closed, reminding me of smiles on death beds, vegetable flesh, maternal earth, and the souls of my departed loved ones. All these men and women have been pursuing one another since the beginning of the world: pimps from strip-tease bars, peddlers of pornographic pictures, madames of small hotels, and the spectators themselves, untroubled tourists. You begin to wonder if they were really alive or were only mannequins that represented every specimen of humanity. What does it matter? They constantly reminded you, by gesture, voice, and glance, at the door of every hotel, bar, and night club, that you were flesh, corruption. Nude bodies wrote in Gothic letters, in streaming light: *thou art dust*. Nuclear acids pour out in torrents. I hear the heart's clock ticking, the hourglass grinding out time, and a tracking shot of death flashes by at supersonic speed. There are only ashes, the same as those

Strozzi used to see on Ash Wednesday when he presided at church ceremonies. Remember that thou art dust. Alleluia, life!

What I was observing was a swarming, wriggling crowd, like a mass of sperm under the microscope, or the torrential blood of the arteries as seen through the eye of the camera. When I looked at the crowd again, I was the reporter of this recognition; it was enough that I knew how to speak and everything was reborn. I was part of this crowd, not much higher than the lowest, a drop of water in the sea. Nevertheless, a prayer was forming in me that I didn't dare express in words. Suddenly I had the sense that in each of these jostled lives, dragged about by forces outside themselves, there was a secret, inalienable zone, invisible to others, an area of the real in which life became more than life. A reflection, that's all that I was.

I was beginning to imitate Strozzi. Was this what he experienced when he walked through the streets at night?

To be attentive, to share in everything except for evil, to search for a meaning, to interpret, to bring form to the formless, *misereor super turbam*, to keep on being attentive — like the person (who was it?) who said at the end of a battle, "No one is dead if I can stand up to sing of this massacre," to give expression to the obscure. I understand, I think I understand, I communicate, I know it all by heart, I am as well acquainted with it as if I were the cause. My wish is that pleasure would emerge and open out onto joy, and that small, everyday pleasures would give way to the great happiness of mid-life, that hope would take root in the hearts of the living. To sing of flesh and blood, its passages that have no exit, and the enormous thrust of pleasure which is the call of God — I think I could do it, while remaining a spectator and a constant transient, if I let myself go. But to stay there, more alone than a star, to visit people, to listen, to help all the actors in the drama, to encourage confidence despite all the evidence against hope, to provide help and go on talking — no, I don't believe I could do that. Right away, I'd start to write, and that would be the end of it. But Strozzi can. All the difference.

A wave of ideas swelled up, flashed out for a second as it bent down, crashed, and scattered in spray, in words, before breaking up. Ideas trickle down on me, from above, from every direction — it's frightening, the way I wallow in ideas. Tomorrow I'll have other ideas, find other words. It doesn't matter. The only thing that counted was that dynamic movement in the depths giving birth to the waves, straining for a happy life, to become invulnerable. To have fewer ideas, to get going, to set out like Strozzi to help someone, to know or not to know on the basis of scientific evidence, and to feel in one's flesh and blood that each drop of water in the sea has infinite importance, even today. To be sufficiently unconcerned with oneself so that each tiny drop comes close . . . .

Me? My friendship is purely literary.

A mist of conscience was all that I was, as I got farther away from the vice district, and the scene of the crowd began to fade, tapering off in the early morning light. A mist of conscience, a little cloud lost among the houses, warm, like vapor from blood, growing, becoming a form, breaking up, contracting, with this kernel at the center — hard, elusive, imperceptible, which tries to assert itself, which says I, which hesitates, refuses, approves, acting as lawyer, judge, or indifferent onlooker, ironic or cold, unless he is listening complacently to the sound of his own voice, or a truth suddenly pierces his heart, a cry lost in the night.

It's strange, this need we have of establishing a reference point, constructing and arranging things so that life won't completely overwhelm us. Once again I had lost my bearings; the world in which Strozzi had been dragging me around for months, like the spectacle I had just seen, was more foreign to me than the world of the Aztecs. Did that mean I felt nothing but contempt for it? But which of us has not experienced the desire to melt into the crowd, to sing with Dionysus? I was all too aware of what my supposed virtue had been like at one time: a fear of the law and public opinion, a fear of harming myself rather than of doing harm, an imitation of the feelings of others, a piety that served to cover up problems rather than throw light on them. At no point did I think of looking down at these people from some lofty perspective. No, my mind was moving in another direction.

I suddenly thought of Maenads I had seen on an ancient sarcophagus near the coast of Naples, or of temples in India, whose statues were juxtaposed, intermingled, unfinished, almost abstract, yet somehow brought back to life, victorious over the formless. As if it was a fearful thing to try to freeze the world in a fixed position, as if the creators of these objects, by refusing to complete an idol, had wanted to indicate that the dynamism of life cannot be controlled and confined as it moves beyond itself. Frenzies of creation or destruction, an attitude of humility and prayer, erotic postures — everything overlapped, as if to suggest that the spiritual life could only exist in flesh that has been subdued. Flesh made up the world of necessity on this vast stage where individuals were only automatons. At the very moment that they believed they were affirming their freedom, they became docile instruments of nature, which used them to organize its game of life and death. In the procession of the Maenads, phallic worship continues from one age to the next: it was simply the song of necessity, an ongoing, eternal effort to bring together what had been divided.

It would have been ridiculous to pretend to superiority. Even purity, in its highest expression, sustained itself with the warmth of blood. It represented the tremendous effort of some individuals to give themselves completely without becoming fragmented. What was the sexual act except the blazing sign of lost unity, the tiny crack that is prophetic of eternity? You will not find yourself in the flesh: that is the judgment that has been pronounced on every love. For it is not the woman he loves that a man encounters in that moment we call possession, but woman, blindly. As if nature were holding out a trap, as if there were some kind of curse on flesh . . . .

Or could it be a great mercy not to be able to find tranquility? Urged on by their thirst for a personal encounter, men and women are dragged into the impersonal cycle of nature and the dynamics of life and death. How does one give life without bringing death? Who has resolved that enigma? Hades and Dionysus were the same god. A sacrament was necessary, a seed of resurrection, so that lovers would stop being afraid, would no longer spy on one another, and together would pass through the gate to the universe of persons.

Those who love one another want proofs. And when the proofs have been given, when they have said "I love you, I love you," with a voice that was only the sigh of the flesh, sometimes nothing more remains of what had been proven except habit, social necessity, and money. When people love each other, they want each other completely, but by devouring one another, they are lost. Woe to someone who wants to know the other completely. Even more wretched is the one who believes he has succeeded!

How do people change from love to hate, silent or declared? I'll tell you, if you don't know. (That's the way things go: ideas flare up and become screams; I summon them up silently, on the deserted streets of early morning.) I hate you because you are not the one I was waiting for, because I am not the one you were waiting for. In the mystery of another kind of love I would have been able to accept you and you would have welcomed me.

What I needed from you was that part of you that is divine, that part of you which is already in the world to come. In reality, I could love you only if I saw that you did not belong to me, only if I clung to what makes you alive. If I want you only in time, as a transient object, you are no more than one of the crowd — used, already old, merely a human specimen, ugly and hateful because you remind me of death. I want to live, and the love that exists beyond you is disappearing. You have been an accomplice, a prostitute, because I only knew how to love you with a fragment of myself.

Life has often given me the privilege of witnessing the miracle of genuine friendship between husband and wife. How I would like to celebrate the splendor of marriage! This miracle can be hidden under the most banal appearances, far from any romanticism, when Eros, even before the weariness and boredom of age, is transformed into gift and begins to radiate light . . . . But marriage doesn't need me to defend it; no one is threatening it, it's in good health, supported by plenty of specialists. But my dear friends, decent churchgoers, I must tell you something that may give scandal. It could be that the depravity which horrifies you may be closer to Love than your faint-hearted love for the human species, than your prudent and stunted love that makes the prodigal son want to get away.

The family is an attempt to arrange natural love. It's a necessary compromise, but in reality it is neither sacred nor final. Paul of Tarsus never saw it in that way either. I'm sorry, or maybe happy, to tell you, if you don't already know, that after we pass through the valley where souls are formed, there will no longer be families, but only persons — that is to say, friends. And woe to you if your wives or your husbands were not friends.

Love is beyond this world; had you forgotten? And if this truth distresses you, remember that it pained me first. Love promises only one thing to those who love with that kind of love: not the ordering of their lives, and not necessarily their sexual comfort, but their own loss--although this loss may turn out to be a gain. Love wants eternity; it is closer to death than to life: nothing can prevent it from sooner or later being crucified. Only friendship comes back to life. But the world does not care for the kind of love which opens up, even here, onto the beyond. Such love is frightening, like everything that is not chained up; it is both liberating and disturbing.

The basic scandal has nothing to do with sexual orgies; everyone is opposed to them; there is almost unanimous agreement. The greater scandal is that love is preached as a tranquil, social wisdom, confusing it with the natural love of family, or with philanthropy. It is not the coupling of husband and wife that the church blesses, my dear parishioners, but the asceticism that marriage implies. Marriage without austerity is the modern form of prostitution. Amen.

My reflections had come to this point. Strozzi's perspective on things had made its way into me. The world of prostitution began to surprise me less. On the stage, in front of the footlights, in a setting appropriate for folklore, this world became, as Strozzi would say, the palpable sign of a more hidden prostitution. It amazed me that a man who carried no weapon, had no protection, was without a system or an impressive list of good works, for twenty years would place himself at — or rather, would let himself be led into — the very center of this human traffic, while the prophetic love in his heart lit up his tanned face.

Once more it seemed obvious to me that it was not to Pigalle that Jerome Strozzi had most to say. It was, rather, to the smooth world of sensible, decent people, of respectable families, to the entrepreneurs of salvation, to those who traded in souls, to all those who prefer money, order and comfort to love. Without knowing or acknowledging it, without ever recognizing it in themselves, they prefer principles to spiritual liberty.

Those were the thoughts that were going on inside me as I walked the deserted streets of early morning, the day before I would have to take leave of Strozzi for a long time. A jumble of consciousness, that's all that it was, all kinds of ideas. I'd have other ideas tomorrow, which would take off in another direction. People shouldn't believe in ideas too much; everything can evaporate in smoke, in words. Yet sometimes it happened that a cry tightened my throat when I thought I'd come upon a small bit of truth, enough to disclose joy for so many people and make the world more friendly. A powerful tenderness would take hold of me as I thought of old Strozzi, dragging himself out at night to see someone, where? No one would be able to protect him from himself any more. Just the evening before the telephone had rung again. For just a second the face of the old fighter had frozen. Then he rushed out headlong to be submerged in the shadows.

"Have you ever thought about your eyes?"

"They'll have everything: liver, spleen, heart, everything. They can do whatever they want to with them. Why do you want me to bother about my eyes?"

"You have to think ahead about eyes. The cornea has to be taken immediately; otherwise, it's too late, and your eyes won't be of use to anyone."

"All right, then. I'll write a new letter to the Dean of the medical school tomorrow morning. After all, I could die suddenly."

Jerome had already written the Dean to donate his body. The Dean had answered with a handwritten letter to thank him, enclosing a card with an address and telephone number. The staff would take care of all the necessary details. Serve life, right to the end: that was Strozzi's idea. Sure, fertilizing the earth was fine, going back into the cycle of carbon; but Strozzi probably thought that the process took too long, what with this obsession of encasing bodies in cement boxes to prevent their mixing with the elements. His boldness would continue beyond the grave.

The idea of writing that letter had come to him that night he had found Eliane behind the red sofa in the luxuriously elegant drawing room on the rue de Longchamp. The medical student whom he had alerted didn't have any shame; he'd already seen what a fine cadaver Eliane would make. Strozzi should have known, he said, that a coma doesn't always prevent someone understanding. "It was an emergency," he said; " they needed cadavers at the medical school."

Eliane was stretched out on the pale blue carpet, everything dislocated, her wrist broken, a fingernail torn out, her face swollen. They were standing, waiting, attentive to the noise in the street. Strozzi seemed fascinated by a golden Christ mounted on green velour in a mahogany frame; it hung above the white marble fireplace. He goes forward a few steps, extends his arm, and grasps it with a sharp twist. Pieces of plaster smash on the fireplace; the Louis XIV clock rolls on the carpet, as the pious frame clanks on the bookcase.

The police would arrive any minute. They would have to tell them something in order to protect the victim, and the criminals who are also victims.

The next morning he had written the letter to the Dean. People like Strozzi are frightening. Let one truth, the tiniest little truth of absolutely no consequence, enter their heads, and it's impossible to get them to let go.

145

"I would so much like to be able to attend my funeral," Strozzi says. "I'd like to see the stupor and frustration on their faces when they come to get the animal when the cortege leaves the church. And then — no Père Lachaise cemetery, the whole ceremony spoiled."

"In fact, you could have sold the . . . . with the money you could have . . . . "

"You know very well that I'm a kept man."

Jerome Strozzi gave me his soul. The good thing about the soul is that you can give it away completely to the multitude, and still keep it . . . . He tells his story then, or rather, lets it be told, torn between his "what's the use?" fear of making a fuss, and his other strong feeling: "If this can help someone to be what he really is, free him to live, why not? After all, they write lots of books on race horses."

At seventy-five, he looks at himself from a distance. Not that he has retired. Every day there's a whirl of letter writing, walks, the subway, elevators, ten hours a day, and more at night. And yet he looks at himself from far away, gently amusing himself with his character.

"I didn't know that about eyes. I'll have to write again. You don't think I'll just be annoying the Dean? I'll write first thing tomorrow morning. Shouldn't put it off."

It really would be a shame if a glance like his didn't shine out again in someone's eyes.